“I HAV

WHERE I AM DROWNING”

A Collection of Humourous Short Fiction

ROB WHITE

I have dreams where I am drowning

Cover Art by Kate Miller

Cover Design by Nathan White

ISBN: 978-1-997713-10-4

Anthologies is an imprint of Pete's Press

I HAVE DREAMS WHERE I AM DROWNING

ROB WHITE

Thanks,

I appreciate you.

ROB WHITE

DEDICATION

This book is dedicated to the people who indulged me creatively when they had absolutely no reason to: Nathan White, Neil Adams, Steve McNeil, Alex Arsenault, Kurtis Rothecker, and John Mailhot.

Special thanks to Kate Miller for her amazing artwork through the years, including the front cover of this book.

TABLE OF CONTENTS

HELL IS PIVOTING TO VIDEO

I won't waste your time with how I ended up in Hell. I'm not here to endure your judgment. I'm here to explain how I've changed Hell—the Brand. Now you might be thinking, "Hell actually exists?" Of course, it does, and entrance is granted far more cheaply than you might think. Statistically, most of us are going to end up burning there forever. It's best not to think about these things, though. Frankly, if you suspect that you're on your way, you probably are. Do you enjoy loud music, or have you ever looked at yourself in the mirror more than once a day? Believe it or not, that's enough. The rules are kind of old school down here.

Once you've accepted that your eternal soul is doomed to an infinite and sometimes perplexing damnation, your next thought might be, "How did you expand Hell as a brand?" When was the last time you heard someone under the age of 50 say, "Go to Hell" or "Damn you to Hell"? You don't hear about Hell anymore. Sure, the word rings loud in chapels and cathedrals, but on the streets of Portland? In the trendy speakeasies of Brooklyn? Like Tower Records or Pan Am airlines, Hell's brand is dead. The Cadillac of damnation is no more. At some point during my daily routine of having pigeons peck out my eyes or waiting for boiling hot tar to be poured on my genitals, the wheels inside my head began to turn. It occurred to me that Hell's population is huge, and it's growing every day. What do you do with miserable people in possession of infinite time and no occupation? You turn them into content creators. And brother, Hell is full of them.

An odd quirk about Hell is its ten-hour work day. You are tortured for ten hours, and then you are more or less free to spend the rest of your time as you please. You can try to sleep, but Hell is, for whatever reason, full of open-air bowling alleys. And if you're lousy at nine ball, there isn't a lot to do but wander around aimlessly. "Put these people to work," I said to myself as I watched my penis melt away under the black tar, only to have it once again regenerate in an equally painful manner. Emboldened by an acute deficiency of human hope, I strolled into the mouth of a large skull that had been carved into the side of an infinitely tall mountain. I assumed, rightfully, that a building so awesomely evil had something to do with the Devil. I chatted up a large bat by the name of Kyle, who turned out to be the Devil's assistant, and I smoothly inquired about the availability of Beelzebub. He wasn't as difficult to get an appointment with as I had imagined, and Kyle penciled me in for a power lunch with Satan for the next day.

I picked out a nice quiet spot overlooking the eighth circle, and I made sure to arrive early. I had pulled together my best-looking tattered rags and used one of the many scorpions lying about to pry the hardened bits of tar that had become affixed to my sallow gray face. "That's probably from all the writhing about while in extreme pain when my penis melts off," I said to myself. I was looking like Hell for sure, but maybe he'd like that? I was feeling nervous until he sashayed in. Graceful, tall, electrifying. After a firm, slightly hot handshake, we shot the shit over a Caesar salad and a few martinis. At one point I called him "Hefe," and he seemed to enjoy that. With a few drinks down the hatch and a smile on his goat-like face, I figured now was as good as any to tell him my plans. Surprisingly, he was quick to agree that Hell was a little behind the times. It was hard even for a de facto CEO not to notice the culture shock that the recently damned had been experiencing. Although my resources were limited, Hell only has one computer, and John Bonham is consistently hogging it in order to google himself. I don't want to disparage the dead, but he really is a fucking piece of shit. Interpersonal issues notwithstanding, my research was top-notch: I produced some of the finest SEO reports and plans, targeted social media strategies, brand awareness, and top-of-mind tips and tricks. Lucifer's head spun when he saw how far down Hell's website had sunk on the Google results. "Page three!" The Son of the Morning bellowed, "Christ's cock, we might as well be MySpace if we're on the third page of search results!" The beast greenlit my plan. It was official: Hell was pivoting to video.

I have a fairly healthy ego (hence my eternal damnation), but there is no way I could have elevated Hell's brand on my own. Up on earth, debilitating rent costs, high unemployment, and a series of brutal snowstorms had sent plenty of hungry, freshly dead marketing and social media experts to Hell, where they fell under my direct supervision. Since you don't need money in Hell, I paid my staff what they coveted more than anything: bootleg NFL jerseys. From time to time, a flaming demon on horseback would distribute them to the groveling masses. I don't understand why it is, but people down here fucking love bootleg NFL jerseys. Kyle the bat helped set up our initial infrastructure. One of the children's torture buildings from the medieval period was renovated and converted into an open-area workspace. Computers, internet lines, and standing desks were brought in. At my direction "fun" elements were added to the office: a swing set and foosball table were added in the middle of the room, and even a few beer taps were installed in the "hangout area" to promote team bonding and to show people "this ain't your granddaddy's Hell." Admittedly, progress was slow at first. Hell's dial-up internet speed limited our aspirations, but eventually Satan became a silent majority partner in a telecom company and the office got fibre. Logos were created by Hell's graphic team (Hell is full of amazing graphic designers), social media accounts were opened, websites were overhauled, and we ordered more swag than we could comprehend: headphones, bags, notebooks, pens with highlighter ends, business cards, and any other cheap piece of plastic you could put a logo on. Unfortunately, the old adage, "You get what you pay for," proved to be apt. The USB thumb drives came preloaded with so much spyware that they were borderline treasonous, and the pens smelt like they had been up some fat guy's ass, which would seem like a crass analogy if you'd never ordered a package from Hell's privatized couriers.

As a content creator, eternal damnation consists of writing the blog on Hell's website. Everything was about getting traffic to the blog. Every "International Puppy Day" or "International Pancake Day" got a blog post with an embedded video. Any puffy, trending news item, celebrity story, or meme got a write-up. We made so many poorly produced "list" videos that even Oskar Schindler dropped a salty comment at my feet in Hell's canteen, and he LOVES lists. The blogs were cross-posted and promoted in ads on Twitter and Facebook, but they never gained any real traction. One day while looking over our disappointing analytics, I realized what we were lacking: the material was there, but none of it spoke to the brand of Hell. Hell is dark, full of flames, and edgy, but our blog had no point of view. It was a regurgitation of whatever had worked elsewhere on the internet. In one sense, this is a sick necessity. The moment you have an opinion, you alienate the broad market and narrow your potential traffic.

"Where are the clicks?" Satan would ask me at our monthly progress meetings. His cool demeanour had fallen away in recent months. I could tell he was beginning to lose faith in the team and, worse, in myself.

"Trust the process," I would tell him, but I was running out of answers and time. Morale had begun to erode in my staff as I pushed them harder and forced them to work longer and longer hours. They had pivoted the blog so many times and in so many directions (even to claymation once, curiously enough) that they no longer knew where the paradigm shift ended and they began. My intense motivational videos, ones where you'd see shots of people in chains and a narrator enticing them to “Break them!” had once empowered them but now had little effect. My jargon was getting more and more ludicrous; one day I used the term “webinar” so many times that, if this was a sane world, there would be a warrant out for my arrest. We were working ourselves to... well, not death but you know. It was bad. The fun elements of the office did little to affect the mood. Nagging injuries from daily torture meant the swing and foosball area were deserted. The beer kegs had been filled with battery acid because, you know, it’s Hell. The break room was never used because breaks were discouraged. The open office concept designed to unite the team had produced the opposite effect. Being robbed of privacy, the staff became paranoid and irritable. The office was hot and uncomfortable, even for a domineering male boss controlling a thermostat in Hell. Times were tough. The chips were down. And when seemingly all hope was lost and we were at the bottom of our emotional barrels, we somehow, inexplicably, went viral.

By the grace of God, our watermark had been superimposed over a video of a man falling down the stairs while carrying a toilet. The video had been seen over 800 million times on various platforms. Sure, I had questions: why was the man filming himself carrying a toilet? How did our watermark get on the video? I wanted to know the answers but there simply wasn’t time. It got likes. It was a gif. It was reposted and regrammed endlessly. Influencers and essential oil entrepreneurs shared it to their drooling followers, who shared it with their ugly families, who, in turn, shared it with their depressive friends and coworkers. It was a "unicorn," a totally unexplainable viral phenomenon that exploded under perfect conditions. And it had the Hell brand all over it.

"Hell is still a thing? Cool," one of the top commenters had said.

Everyone started talking about Hell again. From that point on, every single post we made on every platform got all the likes and clicks we needed to keep the Hell brand top of mind, even though it was the same drivel we had been putting out for months previous. Nothing would ever be as popular as the man with the toilet, but that didn't matter. It's like we entered a dark room, fumbled for months sliding our arms across the walls for a light switch and we had found it completely by accident. We had fortuitously unlocked social media. There was no choice. We had to monetize it.

Within days, we started selling social media marketing services. We would analyze your brand and present a strategy to "enhance your digital presence." We would advise you to get a new logo and start writing blogs. When no tangible results could be seen, we'd say, "Video is the future" to buy a few months of good faith. In reality, the services were thinly veiled vampiristic monthly subscriptions with a costly buyout once you realized we didn't know how to make your brand popular. We would purposely leave out the most crucial element of our success: blind luck.

You've probably seen our clickbait with headlines like "Heaven is not all it's cracked up to be" or "Man is never cold again; find out how!" We created a "troll farm" whose sole purpose was to slag heaven and promote Hell through a tangled web of burner social media accounts with all the facts cited on dubious websites that we would build and fill with false information. That tide had turned. Heaven was out. Hell was in.

But why did I do this? Why did I resuscitate Hell's dead brand? In Hell I ended up earning all of the things I wanted on Earth. In Hell I am powerful, I no longer have a long wait in agonizingly long lines to go bowling. I am popular such that everyone knows my face and my name, from the meager newbie to Mussolini (or Moo Moo as I call him). I am astonishingly wealthy; I have more bootleg NFL jerseys than I know what to do with. And most importantly, in my damnation I found a purpose; a reason to get out of bed. I never felt like I had one on Earth. In Hell I am happy, and I'm going to be here forever. Also, they no longer pour hot tar on my genitals.

I THOUGHT I WAS USING A.I. TO WRITE MY NOVEL BUT IT'S JUST A GUY NAMED AL

I sat down four days ago with an idea, a three-thousand-dollar laptop, and a dream. I was going to write a novel—nah, the Great American Novel. I had it all in my head; I just had to paint the walls, as us writer types say. Sitting in the crowded coffee shop, I let everyone know I was a writer. I laughed and cried along with my characters; I paced with great energy as ideas were hitting me fast and furiously. I typed standing up. We call that writing hard. People watched me, amazed. I said the word "Manuscript" to the barista so many times that he threatened to call the police. And if he would have, I'd have gladly suicided by cop because that's how much I love this shit.

But looking at my work at the end of the day—a day that had felt so fruitful, so full of creativity—I couldn't help but feel crushed. Three hundred forty-seven words. Half a page. I fell into a serious depression; at this rate, my novel wouldn't be done for like a month. And it wasn't just the pace that bothered me; strung together, my words were unreadable gibberish. Ideas that seemed like "can't fail" notions now seemed silly in retrospect. One character named "Broccoli" speaking to another character named "Broccoli"? That's just stupid.

I needed help. I had the three-thousand-dollar laptop, the ideas, but I lacked the ability to sit down and express my thoughts into clearly understandable sentences that would make paragraphs that would make chapters that would tell a story. But how could I fail? I proclaimed myself to be a writer. What else did I have to do? I googled it, and I found my savior: A.I.

"WRITE THE GREAT AMERICAN NOVEL," I put in as my initial prompt. I leaned back and waited. It sure seemed to be taking a long time to get a response. After about ten seconds, I typed a defiant "?" followed by a more prodding "????????"

The system finally spit out a few paragraphs, but it wasn't anything like what I wanted. It appeared to belong to the middle section of a romance novel set in the world of lower-level hockey. The rough around the edges player-coach protagonist had spent the night with a local widow, and he was talking to his fellow players about "catching feelings" for the mourning woman.

"Hm," I said to myself. This isn't about the America I knew anything about. After another moment, the screen filled with a 2300-word sex scene.

"Awesome," I whispered as I took a long haul on my vape.

Days later, I was fully immersed. The prose the A.I. was coming up with spoke with such human grace but was delivered at a speed that was unheard of. Finally, there was nothing between me and my ideas. The pesky middleman that went by the name "Talent" had gone, not to mention his three wise men that always seemed to accompany him:

"Ability," "Concentration," and "Organization." No, not anymore. I had bucked my own trend. Outsmarted my own limitations. "Machine learning," I whispered seductively to myself as I typed in more and more prompts and it responded with more and more sex scenes.

Still, I had my suspicions. It seemed like it was too easy, and that it was still ignoring all of my prompts, no matter how many times I chastised it.

It was time for a test. A softcore Turing test.

My fingers hunted and pecked across the keyboard as I typed the command, "Write a chapter without a sex scene."

For the first time since our initial interaction, the computer was silent for a moment.

"Na," it responded.

I stared at the screen, not used to the machine disobeying.

"Al likes it greasy, baby," it continued.

"NO SEX," I typed back, all caps to get my point across.

"AL LIKES IT GREASY," it responded, full of digital rage.

Wait. AL?

Alright. Some of this is on me. I'll admit that. I didn't use one of those fancy A.I. websites; I used "Yahoo! Chat." An old mainstay in my bookmarks; I've always been able to find everything I need in the Yahoo! family of products. Maybe I should have Asked Jeeves for a better solution, but at the time I wasn't looking for opinions, I was looking for answers. I found a lovely creative chat room called "Al's

Greasy Spot," and I asked a faceless entity for nonrhythmic literature based on my inputs, and he provided hardcore sex scenes couched in between short, mostly pointless scenes of exposition set in the world of minor league hockey. I thought I had wrapped my hands around the reins of the future; instead, I was being dragged hopelessly back into the past.

I closed the Yahoo! Chat window of Al's Greasy Spot. In a huff, I highlighted my text document, and my finger went for the "delete" key. But just before I made contact, I stopped. My eyes skimmed over all the amazing work we had done together. My prompts. Al's words. It was, for a time, the most powerful relationship I've had in years. My finger hovered over the key for some time.

Even years later, I still think of him. Whenever I'm in a new city being ushered from one book signing to another, when I see a minor hockey league team bus or when I flip through a book and come across a 15-page sex scene, I bemoan throwing him away so suddenly. Sure, I went on to bigger things, but did they ever get better than those few initial days with AL? I wanted machine learning, not humanistic regrets. Sitting in the New York Penthouse's Penthouse I bought with the proceeds from my great American novel, I type the same prompt into my fancy A.I. generator over and over:

"2600-word sex scene. 2600-word sex scene. 2600-word sex scene. 2600-word sex scene. 2600-word sex scene. 2600-word sex scene. 2600-word sex scene..."

I'VE BEEN PISSING INTO A SHOP-VAC FOR WEEKS AND NOW I CAN'T STOP

The dulcet tones of "Happy Birthday" were still echoing in the room when my father placed the large box at my feet. The clumsy wrapping paper barely camouflaged what was inside. It had been a while since either of my parents had wrapped a gift so large and imposing. I was 34, after all, far past the age for such grandiose offerings. You didn't have to wrap a gift card or a nice lunch at a medium-priced restaurant. I tore off the wrapping paper and uncovered the darkest phase of my life: a brand-new Shop-Vac.

"Don't piss into it," my father said sternly, his eyes holding mine with a long, morose stare. He was a serious man; this was a serious request. Everyone around the table, my brothers, my mother, was silent. The thought hadn't even entered my mind, and now it felt like it would never leave.

I had never felt as torn between my ideas of "right" and "wrong" as I was in those initial days. The box sat in the corner of the living room of my bachelor suite. I covered it with towels and spare bedding, but the bottom left corner of the box peeked out, touting its "Super Sucking Action." What a tease. On the third day, with my hands shaking, my bladder filling, and the blood in my veins rushing to my head like the great Mississippi, I sliced open the packing tape and pulled out the impressively sized cylindrical aluminum body.

I feel that I must clarify something to you. I'm not some *weirdo*. I don't have a neckbeard. My girlfriend is not a large pillow adorned with an anime character. I am typical. You probably wouldn't notice me on the street, let alone in a sparse subway train car. I work in a marketing department where I liaise between the creative types and the accounts people. I am good-natured and am well-liked by my co-workers. I have had what I think is a normal amount of relationships that have lasted for a fairly normal amount of time. I am by no means a neat freak, but I am also not a slob. I am decidedly normal, almost to a fault. I have never pissed into anything in my house aside from my toilet. Until. Until...

While assembling the Shop-Vac, I kept telling myself all the cleaning I would accomplish with it. "I could get all the grit out of the BBQ, tidy up after whatever woodworking projects I decide to tackle, really, and I mean really clean the rugs of my car; also I can piss into it"—NO. I chastised myself for the thought. I tightened the last screw and took a step back to admire the finished product. "Wow," I said out loud. The buckle of my belt banged loudly on the tiles as my pants fell to the floor.

The feeling was one that is hard to describe. I've never felt so empty. So totally satisfied with the act of urination. Every drop was gone, accounted for. I no longer felt the need to use any other bathroom. Why waste it? Nothing on that puny urinal was even measured in horsepower like my Shop-Vac. "No thanks, I'll hold it," I told people who noticed me grinding my teeth, sweating profusely, and shaking my leg. Letting loose a downright frightening torrent of urine into your Shop-Vac after a long day of work was what I imagined it was like to pray for your entire life and finally hear the voice of God.

I had never realized before how much time I was wasting getting up and using the bathroom. By simply keeping the Shop-Vac at my side at all times, I had opened up a magical door of endless productivity. My ideas were coming fast and furious. I'd fire off emails at all hours of the night, much to the chagrin of my co-workers whose effort level, when compared to mine, made it seem like they were spending their whole days walking to and from the bathroom.

"I'm so proud of you and all you're able to accomplish," my mom said into the phone. My big toe hovered over the power switch of the Shop-Vac, anxious for the conversation to end.

"You're so much like your father. Like the world has more hours in the day for both of you." We said our goodbyes, and I hung up the phone and evacuated into the Shop-Vac's welcoming nozzle attachment.

But that sentence stuck with me. *Like the world has more hours in the day for both of you.* I recalled a memory of my father. It was a warm autumn day that seemed to be tinted gold. I was just a boy. We had been out for a long drive, and my leg shook like crazy. I was desperately trying to calm my swelling bladder, and soon enough, I noticed my father doing the same. The truck had barely come to a stop, and I was already across the lawn and pulling at the fly of my jeans. I remember looking back at my father, who was gingerly walking to the garage. Even though I felt like I was going to burst, I stopped to watch this man, my hero, disappear into the detached garage. Before continuing into the house, I remember the muffled sound of some kind of motor. I thought it had been a distant lawn mower, but now I understand

I had a weird feeling. Later, in my storage unit I began searching through the gigantic box that the Shop-Vac came in and I found a note. It was in my father's handwriting.

"Don't forget to take out the filter."

Today, my boss applauded the extra effort I had been putting in at work and hinted that I might be in line for a large promotion. "Private Bathroom," he said, lifting his eyebrows. I just hope it has a grounded outlet. I was a Shop-Vac man, and nothing was ever going to change that now.

THE WHEEL OF TIME — MY LITERARY PRISON

The judge brought the gavel down and I'm not too ashamed to say that I was shaking. I nervously ran my hands through my hair. My only crime had been curiosity and yet here I was, in this courtroom fighting for freedom. One of the jurors, a petite woman in a yellow floral print dress, wept loudly. The man beside her had been trying to calm her down for the better part of the last ten minutes, but to no avail. She blew her nose into a ratty Kleenex. Her words were separated by deep, painful-sounding gasps:

"Nobody. Deserves. This."

Guilty. Guilty on all counts. The judge shook his head as he stared at the sentencing recommendation. When he read it aloud, everyone gasped: the spectators in attendance, the lawyers *on both sides* of the case, and even the grizzled bailiff, Terry.

I was condemned to read the entire *Wheel of Time* series. All 14 books. eleven thousand pages. 4.1 million words. This was to be my literary prison. One time. Doing time. For a long time.

I wasn't sure what to expect, but it was a lot like house arrest. The sheriff's office came to my home and stripped it of all entertainment. Video game consoles, laptops, televisions, smartphones, and even the other books on my shelf were hauled away. Before boxing it up, one of the sheriffs looked at the complete *Dark Tower* series by Stephen King sitting on my shelf. “Looks like you’ve done some hard time before, huh?” the officer said, poking at *Wizard and Glass* with a pencil, before shoving the entire shitty collection of books into a box. I was left with a primitive Motorola Razr for phone calls and the three large boxes that the authorities had left in the middle of my living room floor. As I signed for the contents of my lengthy sentence, I asked the man who handed me the clipboard, “So, is it good? The series, I mean.”

“It’s really long... So... it’s long” he responded.

“I can do this,” I told myself. Before they hauled away my computer, I managed to do a bit of research on the series, and I broke it down as such: if I read 75 pages a day, I would finish the series and get my life back in five months. With nothing else to do for entertainment, nothing else to occupy my time, I could certainly read at least 75 pages a day. Maybe even 200. I opened the boxes, arranged the mammoth books on my shelf and cracked the spine of “The Eye of the World.”

“You haven’t gotten through much, huh?” the deputy remarked to me, going over my court-appointed biweekly reading log. It’s true. After a few days of what I thought was good progress, I stumbled. The last time I tried to read, I found myself tipping the spine forward to examine how much I had read and how much was left. It didn’t seem possible. The endless descriptions. The meticulous details. The unending procession of characters. The lengthy asides. The creeping suspicion that this story is just a really long version of *Star Wars*. I put the book down, stared at the wall and tried to imagine a universe that wasn't so cruel.

I weakly grabbed at the deputy's arm as he got up to leave. He was the only person I'd seen in the flesh since my ordeal had begun. He looked at my hand in disgust and then up into my desperate eyes.

"Audiobooks?" I asked meekly.

His face didn't change; he looked at me like I was a criminal. I suppose he saw me as I was.

"You don't *read* the radio," he cruelly whispered through clenched teeth. He shook my hand off his arm and left the house.

He was right. You don't read the radio.

The deputy must have reported the audiobook comment, because the next day I was picked up and driven a few hours to a state facility. By the evening, I found myself in a beige jumpsuit, being escorted down a long hallway by two apprehensive-looking guards. There was a strange, specific smell in the air.

"Is that...the smell of second-hand books?" I asked the guard.

"I dunno, man," he replied. "I've been here so fuckin' long I don't even notice anymore."

The corridor was lined with cells. An old, bearded man stared at me hard as I passed by, his cell floor littered with various volumes of the *No. 1 Ladies' Detective Agency*. It was a chilling vision of my future. Two guards ran down the hall, almost knocking me over as they passed. They yelled into their radios about a suicide attempt in the *Anna Karenina* wing.

The cell door softly latched behind me. I sat down on my bed and in the distance I could hear, just above the sound of the soft turning of pages from adjacent cells, an overloaded book cart grinding against the concrete floor as two men laboriously pushed it down the same corridor I had just walked. I knew what it was. My sentence. One page, one chapter, one book at a time.

I don't know what kind of world will be out there for me when I finish the Wheel of Time. I'm not sure I remember what the world was like when I left. But finishing the books isn't the end. It's not that simple. Going door to door, telling my new neighbours that I am a registered *Wheel of Time* completionist. Their looks of revulsion. Humiliating background checks for menial jobs. The pain when an old friend won't pick up the phone. The feeling of not knowing where to begin my new life. Maybe it's better here, easier. There is no one to look me in the eye and let me down. Maybe it's better to not finish *The Wheel of Time*.

THE CLASSICS

Arthur deserved a vacation, like anyone else. All he wanted was some time to himself, a few days to unwind at the family cabin, lounging in the sun, relaxing, and reading some of his favourite books. The classics. And now he's tied to a chair. And the rain. The pissing rain.

He had hit the road early to make the most of the day. The clouds started looking ominous as he sped down the desolate grid roads halfway into the three-hour drive.

"Shit," Arthur mumbled. By the time he had descended the road to the lakefront property, the rain was coming down hard. Oh well. He could read inside just as well as outside. All he needed was privacy. Perhaps the weather would even deter the hill people.

"Hill people" was a term of derision by which Arthur referred to the new money folk who had invaded his family's beach community. They had begun arriving ten years ago and had continued to arrive in droves ever since. They bought up lots and old rundown properties, erecting gaudy cabins. No, not cabins. These were houses. They filled every square inch of their property with boats and quads. Keeping up with the Joneses, he who dies with the most toys wins, etc... This was ironic because they spent most of their time watching TV thanks to the satellite dishes that hung like new brutalist gargoyles on their capitalist cathedrals, or so Arthur thought.

But the one thing they didn't have, the one thing they couldn't buy, the one thing they wanted more than anything in the world was his: lakefront property. The view made them crazy, but the term "lakefront" made them crazier. Lately, however, they had been encroaching.

First, it was Mr. Granger, the drunk. Someone had paid him $100,000 for his lot, the same lot he had paid $10,000 for in 1962. Sure, he had a "lakefront" property, but only technically. His view was miserable, and the entrance was on the corner of a dangerous hairpin turn.

As for Arthur's cabin, his dad had purchased it from his own father for $25,000 20 years ago. Arthur's dad used to muse aloud about selling the cabin outside the family, but Arthur's impassioned pleas always changed his mind. Not that Arthur particularly liked the outdoors or even the cabin itself, but more so he revelled in whining to get his way and did so whenever he got the chance.

It seemed like every weekend one of the hill people would slime their way down the road. Arthur could see them fantasizing, no doubt, about where they would park their jeep and place their security cameras. Often, Arthur would go tell them off, but he found that talking to his neighbours was akin to having his brain take a shit. Sports stats, Hollywood blockbusters, and celebrity gossip. That's all they knew. Arthur couldn't talk to the hill people about anything that mattered. Art. Literature. The Classics.

Pulling into the beach community, Arthur stared with contempt at all the perfect homes. He hoped all of this rain would wash them away. The rain was coming down in sheets as Arthur pulled up to the driveway of the humble family cabin. Even though it was midday, between the gloomy sky and heavily wooded lakefront road, it was unusually dark.

He grabbed his suitcase out of the trunk of the car and turned to make his way to the front door, but something, some feeling, stopped him in his tracks. He turned to see that someone was watching him from the road. A tall man, he presumed, in a dark rain slicker. The baggy hood of the slicker covered his face. Arthur was relieved at first, but the stillness of the figure in the rain made him feel uneasy.

"Hey, how are you?" Arthur called out to the figure. The person didn't reply. He just stared. The rain was coming down hard around him.

"Looks like I brought the bad weather with me, huh?" Arthur quipped, holding his suitcases up. He almost hated himself for resorting to banal small talk, but he was unnerved. The figure glanced at Arthur's luggage. Arthur turned on his heels and hastened to the front door of the cabin. He had the impression that the figure was just behind him, breathing down his neck as he fumbled with the deadbolt lock.

The door finally opened, and Arthur spilled into the entranceway, but when he turned to close the door, there was no one there. Just the pissing rain pooling on the rotten boards of the porch.

"Fucking hill people," Arthur said, feigning confidence. He slammed the door shut and locked it. Throwing open the shades of the large deck windows, Arthur was greeted not by a glorious view but by the darkened reflection of himself, all 140 pounds of him, damp and breathing heavily. Wiping the rain off his glasses, Arthur indulged in a violent reimagining of his encounter with the figure on the road. Of course, he would have overcome the man; there was no doubt in his mind of that. Arthur was, after all, the noble hero in the story in his head, beset on all sides by enemies; he was due his inevitable deserts. A character that would fit perfectly in one of his classics.

He shook his head at the thought and made his way into the master bedroom off the living room. Tucking his suitcase under his bed, he felt tired. The drive had been exhausting, and the adrenaline from his encounter was wearing off. He could barely make it into the bed, its weakened old springs creaking under his slight frame.

"I should read," he thought to himself lamely as he fell into a deep sleep. Unknown to him, in the pouring rain on the deck, the figure in the rain slicker cupped his hands around his eyes and peered through the deck windows. He stared at the suitcase under Arthur's bed.

Arthur woke a few hours later to the sound of rain outside. It was starting to make him nervous. The torrential rain poured hard on the old cabin, loudly spilling over the overwhelmed eavestroughs and onto the dirt below. The incessant patter left little room for the thoughts in his head.

Lying in bed, he tried to think about what he should do next. "I should read," Arthur repeated to himself, straining to get up. Leaning down, he grabbed his suitcase and laid it on the bed. The suitcase was vintage, probably from the sixties, and bright baby blue. Sure, it was harder on the back and shoulder to lug around than the newer rolling luggage, but he thought it made him look interesting. It did not. It made him look like an asshole, but Arthur had long ago alienated both those who would be nice enough and those who would be cruel enough to tell him that.

As he reached for the clasp, a loud crack of thunder boomed outside. Instinctively, he turned his head to the deck windows. A flash of lightning illuminated the outside. Arthur froze. He couldn't have been sure, but out of the corner of his eye he thought he saw someone standing on the deck. Before he could investigate, there was a crash from the front of the cabin. Arthur shot up to his feet and stuffed the suitcase back under his bed. He grabbed a childish-looking yellow raincoat from the closet and hustled to the front door. He returned to the living room an instant later, surveyed his options, and grabbed a golf club.

Arthur stood outside staring at the cause of the loud crash. An eavestrough overwhelmed by the rain had been torn off of the cabin and crashed to the ground. Nothing more sinister than that. The rain. The pissing rain did this. The figure in the window? The figment of an overactive imagination. Too many long nights spent reading the classics. The thought made Arthur pause. He couldn't recall a night in recent memory that he had actually sat down and read any of the books. But he must have. Shaking himself from the disquieting thought, Arthur did his best handyman impression, reconnecting the eavestrough to the cabin with a pair of bungee cords. This kind of thing was never his forte. It might not last forever, but it was repaired for now. Most importantly, Arthur, now wet and tired, felt that he had earned an evening of reading. Back in the bedroom, dry and warm, Arthur stared at the closed suitcase on the bed. He bounced his fingers over the clasps. He let out a slow breath. If he started reading now, he might get too wrapped up, and by the time he pulled himself away, it would be too late to make a quality dinner.

Pulling open the vintage fridge door, Arthur was smacked across the face by the smell of rotten food. The eggs and milk had gone bad and the meat looked suspicious. He hadn't been to the cabin in a couple of weeks. What had he been expecting to find?

"Time to visit the hill people," Arthur sneered through his teeth.

Arthur's '97 Camry struggled up the incline of the lakefront road but after a few dodgy moments, he was cruising down Main Street past the beautiful new homes on the hill. Having arrived early, he had been spared seeing any of the dopey hill people's faces but now, in the early evening, they had all gotten off work and made their way into the community. Somehow his neighbours had pulled their faces from their televisions and iPads, so Arthur was forced to suffer their stares and quiet scorn. They look disgusted. Disgusted at him. At his disgusting car. The idea that *this* disgusting person enjoys lakefront property.

The general store was at the top of the hill across from the beach. It was nothing special, offering boxed groceries and a few fresh items. While browsing, Arthur spotted a mini community library set up on a table in the corner of the store. A paper sign read, "take-a-book, leave-a-book." Arthur couldn't resist finding out what the philistines were reading, or at least what they had attempted to read three years ago before giving up on page 20. As he rummaged through the titles, his cynicism was vindicated. It was your typical schlock: romance novels, books adapted to films, and children and youth novels. But, amidst the trash, Arthur noticed something. Gravity's Rainbow by Thomas Pynchon. One of the classics.

"Amazing. An amazing novel," Arthur said just loud enough for someone in the store to hear him. Flipping it open, he revelled in the first line of the novel, "A screaming comes across the sky," Arthur gushed, with a mawkish tone. He turned to the second page and in the corner there was a crude drawing of a muscular man. Arthur was outraged. Who would do this? This is one of the classics. He flipped to the next page and the muscular man was there again; this time his right hand had slid down to his noticeably shorter shorts. On the third page, the hand began undoing the zipper on the muscular man's shorts. Arthur, now furious, began to turn the pages of the book faster, animating the crude flip book, which ended with the muscular character ejaculating all over the text of page 23.

"Animals. Filthy animals," Arthur mumbled to himself. He paid for his groceries and, full of self-righteous determination, stomped out into the rain and to his car

Driving back to the cabin, Arthur noticed that something had drawn the hill people out of their homes. They were wearing seemingly identical rain slickers, staring expressionlessly as he drove by. Arthur recalled his encounter with the creepy figure in the rain slicker and what he thought he had seen from the corner of his eye on the deck before the eavestrough broke. The way these hill people were staring at him was making him uncomfortable. Sure, he was going a little fast, but that's what they got for staking giant signs on the side of the road with hysterical slogans like, “PLEASE SLOW DOWN, WE LOVE OUR CHILDREN.” Arthur always wondered what he was meant to assume about the cities, towns, and beach communities with no such reminders.

“They love their children, too. They don’t have to go on about it all the goddamn time," Arthur mumbled to himself. The rain and humidity, fighting the heat from his body, had begun to fog up the inside of the windshield. Arthur tried to engage the heating/cooling system, wrestling with the concept in his head while randomly pushing buttons. Giving up, he wiped the fog with the sleeve of his shirt just in time to see that he was about to plow into a group of hill people. Arthur stomped on the brakes hard and his Camry skidded to a stop.

“Jesus,” he growled, his heart pounding. A flicker of shame rose in him as he peered through the still-fogged window. The hill people didn’t seem to notice how close they’d come to being run down. They just stood there in identical rain slickers and stared at him as the rain came down around them. After a moment they began to shuffle out of the middle of the road. Arthur, feeling compelled to say something, rolled down his window.

“I’m, uh, sorry about that. The windows are pretty fogged up and uh...” At once all of the hill people turned towards him. Those furthest from Arthur began to whisper amongst themselves. One of the hill people calmly walked towards the car. Arthur smiled the kind of smile you give someone just after you narrowly avoided killing them, but the person was now getting uncomfortably close to the car. He was an older man. Instinctively Arthur began to roll up the window but was forced to stop when the strange man put his hand on the windowpane.

"Slow down. We love our children," the man said in a monotone. He smiled, turned around and walked away. Arthur quickly rolled up the window.

"Fucking hill people," he said to himself, putting the car into drive and continuing down to the cabin.

After a nice dinner, Arthur once again found himself staring at the unopened suitcase.

"Hmm." If he started reading now, no doubt Arthur would be sucked into one of the classics, and, before he knew it, it would be god knows what time. "It's been a long day. I'll start fresh in the morning," he concluded.

The rain never stopped pouring as Arthur had hoped, all through the night. He awoke tired, and after a small breakfast, sat staring at the suitcase again. Anxiously, he tapped his fingers on its hard top, as if he were safeguarding state secrets or concealing a dangerous weapon.

"Maybe I'll go for a walk. Clear my head," Arthur said to himself.

Arthur had always felt the best while he was on the trail. The trail was a shortcut that led to the beach from the lakefront road by way of a densely wooded area. Normally, the trail was secluded, but this time Arthur felt he was not alone. He felt eyes on him almost immediately once he had left the main road. His mind went back to the man with the slicker in front of the cabin. He shivered. The rain was so heavy that it was hard to hear anything save for the sound of it smacking on his jacket. His glasses had begun to fog. If someone had been following him, he was easy prey: virtually deaf and blind.

The trail was in bad shape. In good conditions, it only took ten minutes to reach the beach, but he was roughly 20 minutes into the journey, his orientation lost as if he'd been spun around. The path was not a straight walk and required him to cut through a few neighbour's properties (clearly marked "Private"). Arthur had become absorbed by the hill people's various crimes against his personal humanity when, while absentmindedly crossing a semi-steep slope, he immediately lost his footing in the wet mud. He fell on his side and, failing to grab at any of the vegetation, he rolled for some time down an embankment, landing on his back with a hard 'thud.'

Winded, dazed, and defeated, Arthur lay there for a moment with the rain pelting his face. His glasses were gone, and it would take a miracle to get back to the cabin in this state. Over the sound of the pounding rain, and an overture of self-pity, Arthur heard something: heavy footsteps, the kind that come from professional galoshes. The kind a seasoned hunter would wear.

Craning his neck toward the sound, he spotted a blurry mass a few meters away. A figure in a slicker looked down on him, its face obscured by the hood. Raising his arm, Arthur weakly pleaded, "Please. Please help me." The figure cocked its head at Arthur like a puzzled dog. Arthur let his hand fall to the ground and passed out.

The rain. The pissing rain.

That's how Arthur found himself tied to a chair in the living room of the family cabin. He only had a vague sense of how he had arrived: The backseat of a car. His ribs digging into a stranger's shoulder blade. The feeling of being carried, one he hasn't experienced since he was a child. Now here he was, his wrists and ankles painfully fastened to the ancient wooden chair. His head hung limply forward. When he managed to pick it up and look around, he found he was surrounded by eight people in identical rain slickers, their faces hidden. It sounded like the bedroom was being ransacked.

"You find it?" one of the men in the rain slicker called toward the bedroom.

"No. Nothing yet," the voice replied.

"Under the bed," another one called, this time a woman's voice.

"Why didn't you say that in the first place?" the voice from the bedroom grumbled. "I found it!"

There was an anxious moment as the person fumbled with something in the bedroom. The group of slicker-clad figures murmured amongst themselves. Arthur was puzzled as to what was happening until he heard the familiar click of his vintage suitcase clasps. The group fell silent. *What did these people want with his books?* Arthur thought.

"Fuck!"

The man exploded out of the bedroom and launched the contents of the suitcase onto the floor in front of Arthur.

"Where is it?" The man screamed into Arthur's face.

"Where's what?" the words meekly leaving his mouth.

"The low-pressure system! The showers! The arctic air!" The man was screaming now.

"The gale force winds," the woman in the rain slicker added helpfully.

"Unrelenting precipitation!" Another man yelled. Arthur's eyes shifted back and forth trying to keep up with the people screaming at him. He was confused and terrified. Perhaps he was concussed or hallucinating. The man who had thrown the suitcase on the floor picked up two random books, Ulysses by James Joyce and Infinite Jest by David Foster Wallace, and began shaking them angrily in Arthur's face.

"This....unreadable garbage was all we found!" The man yelled, soaking Arthur's face with spit.

"The classics?" Arthur asked. The group of rain slickers grew more impatient.

"Where is it?!" one of them yells.

"Yeah. Where the hell did you hide it!" another called out.

One of the rain slickers, who had to this point been standing toward the back of the room, smoothly stepped forward. Looking at the imposing outline, Arthur now believed this was the figure he had seen when first arriving at the cabin. The figure produced a large buck knife from under his slicker and held it to Arthur's cheek. Calmly and no louder than a whisper, the voice of a man emanated from the slicker's black, faceless void.

"Where is it?"

"WHERE IS WHAT?!" Arthur screamed into the man's face, this time dousing the accuser with his own spit. Everyone froze. For a moment, the only sound in the room was the rain pounding against the roof.

"The bad weather, Arthur." the large figure hovering over him said calmly. Arthur was confused. "The other day you stood out there in the driveway and told me that you brought the bad weather with you. Why!? Why did you do this to us!?" The man exploded, digging the edge of the buck knife into Arthur's cheek. "If it keeps raining, all of these cabins are going to fall into the lake! Why are you doing this to us?" The man screamed at a volume that made his words almost difficult to distinguish.

"It was just-" Arthur shook with fear, unable to get the words out of his mouth.

"JUST WHAT?!"

"It was just an expression." The words finally escaped Arthur's mouth. He began to softly weep, a small trickle of blood running down his cheek.

The man with the knife took a step back and looked at the group of rain slickers. They shared a moment in silence.

"Oh," the man with the knife replied flatly. "Ohhh!" The group of rain-slicked figures began to laugh. They pulled the hoods of their slickers down, revealing their faces. Arthur looked at them one by one, shocked by their complete ordinariness. All of them in their forties and fifties, all of them so suburban.

"That's why you kidnapped me? Over a turn of phrase?" An exhausted Arthur managed to ask.

"You know how it is," the man with the knife said with a measure of humility. "As soon as you drove in, the rain started. I came down here to make sure you got down the hill all right because your car looks like a *real* piece of shit, and you said the thing about "bringing the bad weather," which I thought was *weird*. So I hopped on the community's Facebook chat and made mention to Tom and Mavis... then the signal for our satellite dishes all went out and the Wi-Fi died... I guess we just all got a bit carried away. Honestly, we had nothing else to do."

"I don't believe this!" Arthur exclaimed. Enraged, he pulled hard with his feet and hands but couldn't budge out of the chair. "You fucking stupid hill people!"

"Hey, hey, we don't appreciate that," said the man with the knife. "That nickname."

"That's a term of derision," one of the female former slickers said with scorn in her voice.

"Three syllables. Wow! Where'd you learn that one, Helen, your word of the day app?" Arthur shouted in a mocking tone.

"You know what?" The woman began, moving closer to Arthur, speaking the way a schoolteacher would to a disruptive student. "You think you're so darn smart with these books." She pushed a newly translated hardcover copy of Finnegan's Wake out of her path with her foot. "Well, let me tell you, mister, the only thing you're going to find in these pretentious, unreadable books that people hold up in such high regard is a false sense of superiority. And if I was a betting woman, which I am not, good Lord no, I would bet that you spent all weekend finding excuses to not open a single one of these books."

The crowd of rain slickers agreed audibly, almost breaking out into a full-blown cheer. The woman's voice grew gentler. Arthur can't hide the shame on his face.

"You know, if you have problems finding the motivation to read, you should maybe try to read something a little funner"

"Maybe a lighthearted fantasy novel or even a biography on someone interesting that you like," the man with the knife offered.

"Sometimes if I am in a rut, I try to read something short, just to get me back in the habit of reading. Set some page goals and work from there."

"Don't get too discouraged if a book isn't right for you. Don't feel guilty over it, just move on," another voice added.

"If you're really stuck, there is nothing wrong with young adult novels. Lots of good authors that are sometimes overlooked due to the genre," another voice called out. Arthur's head was spinning. He couldn't believe he was getting advice from the people who'd tied him to a chair. Hill people.

"I don't need your reading advice! I'm not going to read young adult novels. I need you rich fucking truck-driving yokels to untie me from this goddamn chair!" Arthur yelled, quieting everyone in the room.

“Cut him loose, Jerry. I guess killing him won’t stop the rain after all,” one of the men in the rain slickers acknowledged with disappointment in his voice. Arthur was shocked but thought it unwise to complain any more than he already had.

Jerry approached Arthur with the intention of cutting him loose, but just as he came within reach, there was a sudden crash from the front of the house. He turned violently toward the sound of the clatter and in doing so inadvertently slashed Arthur’s throat with the buck knife. The crowd of rain slickers gasped in unison. The chair, with Arthur still affixed, fell to the floor. Having severed his carotid artery, Arthur began to bleed profusely. One of the rain slickers ran to inspect the crash.

“Looks like the eavestrough gave out!” He shouted back to the group. “Someone did a piss-poor job with this thing.”

“It’s not really my forte,” Arthur managed to gurgle out as he bled to death. He watched his blood pool under a copy of The Trial by Franz Kafka, no doubt ruining it. “The...Classics”. As Arthur loudly expelled his last breath, the rain outside stopped.

Arthur’s captors watched this unfold in disbelief.

“Well,” the woman who gave Arthur the lecture began, looking out at the now calm weather, “I think that... solves...that”. The others nodded solemnly.

The sky began to brighten as the sun peeked out from behind the clouds. Everyone turned and looked out the large deck windows, admiring the beautiful view of the lake.

"Wow," Jerry said after a moment of quiet. "I would kill for a view like that". Everyone nodded in agreement.

Then the cabin began to shake.

"What's happening?" someone yelled. But it was already too late. Chaos overcame the cabin as furniture and people began to topple over each other. The cabin upended itself entirely and slid down the steep embankment and into the lake, killing everyone inside.

Later, the civil engineers would report that they'd never seen anything like it. The area had never experienced so much rain in such a short period. The excess moisture had eroded the soil just under the main supports of the cabin, which caused it to topple into the lake. One engineer supplied the epitaph "Kafkaesque," which of course didn't describe the situation at all, but it sounded pretty smart. Who could read those books anyway?

MY FAVOURITE SHIRT HAS LEATHERFACE GIVING YOU THE FINGER

It's been with me through good days, bad days, and the ones so ordinary you end up forgetting about them altogether. My favourite shirt has seen them all.

I remember the first time I saw it. I was flipping through Truck Progression Magazine, October 2001. Like many of us, I was trying to find my way through the haze that 9/11 had left us all in. I needed a shakeup. My wardrobe was drab. No one ever looked at me, negatively or positively. No one seemed to see me at all. I merely existed, and had I not noticed myself, I would have failed to exist at all.

Far from the glossy spreads of powerful trucks colliding with pits of mud, the t-shirts offered on that cheap newsprint in the back pages began to pique my interest:hardline confederate flags and Black Sabbath logos dotted the pages, but this wasn't the "new me." I wasn't going to be a bigot or some overly nostalgic rock fan; I was going to be something new. Something shocking.

I turned the page—and there it was. The beginning of the new me: horror character Leatherface, donning a mask made of human skin, holding his trademark chainsaw in his right hand while brandishing the middle finger on his left.

I placed the order the next day.

Weeks passed, but I didn't watch the mailbox or wait for the delivery man with bated breath. I was already different. I was already wearing the t-shirt inside. I was Leatherface, flipping the bird wherever I went. Things began to change for me. I spoke with confidence. I unconsciously demanded eye contact, and people couldn't help but make and keep it.

One afternoon at the mall, I was asked to attend a test screening for Blue Crush. I was no longer fighting to exist. I was thriving.

I arrived home from an important meeting to find a package on my front step.

It was time. No more theories.

I tore open the parcel. I slipped the shirt onto my body, and I actualized. Yet there is a cost for wearing such an excellent t-shirt. I became the lone wolf. With the garment came the disdain. The stares. The whispers. There were no more movie screenings, meetings, or eye contact. There was me and the shirt.

"Do you have to wear it every day?" Some would ask me.

"Yes. Yes, I do. It's my favourite shirt," I would reply.

You could say, and some have, that the shirt has made my life harder. As though it's an unnecessary obstacle to employment, respect, and co-mingling. But what they don't understand is: what is a shirt if it is not worn? To exist to sit in a dark closet or a drawer. To hear the world going on around them but to be shut away. That's not the life for my favourite shirt. Yes, the funerals have been awkward. The job interviews have not been favourable. Suit and tie? Business casual? I think the Leatherface on my t-shirt will let you know what I think about them. I was forced to see movies like everyone else - without giving any notes at the end like some kind of everyday loser.

It is still in impeccable condition. The care. The responsibility. The weight of being the caretaker for such a garment is its own reward. This shirt is my lifeline to my youth because no one leaves this world in immaculate condition.

The people around me are not like t-shirts. Friends, family, and colleagues. Their stains are on the inside. Their wear and tear don't show under the armpits or on the hems but on their faces. And soon enough, when they are faded and worn out, their graphics cracked and peeling, they are taken away to a big donation bin in the sky.

But my favourite shirt survives.

Unstained. Untorn. If you didn't know better, you would say that it has never been worn. Yes, it is rarely laundered and yes that is what the “Jefe”-sized can of Axe Cool Fire bodyspray is for. But here is my favourite shirt, tucked into my jeans, khakis, or dress pants at every milestone for the past 20 years. It has seen many enter and leave our lives, and barring some miracle, it will see many more.

So every day, I open the closet and pull my favourite shirt off of its hanger and slip it on. Just like I did yesterday. Just like I will tomorrow. Just like I will for all the ones so ordinary that you end up forgetting about them altogether.

"Fuck you and fuck this," says the Leatherface on my t-shirt.

Indeed.

ADVENTURES IN MICRODOSING THE POLICE FORCE

Deep down, do you really want to ask questions? Isn't it infinitely more comforting to live with the answers we have, even if they are the wrong ones? If only I had the foresight to understand that a few weeks ago before I started micro-dosing everyone at the police station that I work at.

The idea seemed right at the time, and like so many decisions I'd later come to regret, it had come to me under a time of duress. Everyone in the station seemed so tense all the time. There were a lot of heated exchanges behind closed doors. Things had become a little right-wing for my taste. You could feel it in the common area, it was a bad vibe, and I don't do bad vibes. I actually own a hilarious shirt that says as much. I knew I had to change things, and after I had been laughed out of my boss's office for suggesting the installation of a nap room, I knew that I had to be a little underhanded about it.

I had been complaining about the heavy atmosphere to my good friend Maze when he had a brilliant suggestion. Maze had been battling a serious case of depression since recently losing his entire leather pants collection in a blades-related stovetop fire, but he found that he had cured his case of blues by micro-dosing psilocybin mushrooms. He claimed that in just a few weeks, his mood began to lighten, fears and anxieties felt "washed away," and he was able to turn a few pairs of the once thought-to-be-ruined leather pants into leather shorts.

"Hmm," I wondered, staring at the leather shorts. "What could be the downside of a collective mood change in a small town's only police detachment?"

Free of angst and worry, imagine the change we could make not only within ourselves but also in our community.

Maze was kind enough to act as the middleman between myself and the fungiculturist, who he called his "mushman." We were able to meet up with him forthwith in his mobile office, a 1993 Econoline van. The invisible hand of the market dictated that I had to go a little deeper into my coffers than I felt comfortable with, but Maze assured me that the shit was "good" and that those squares would get "goofy as hell." I once again reiterated my mission statement to de-stress and slowly evolve the vibe state, but Maze and his mushman had grown preoccupied with the number of purple hairs on a bud of marijuana and were no longer listening to me.

As for a delivery apparatus, I figured that the best way to cover the ghastly flavour of the mushrooms was to steep them in the communal morning coffee. I was able to get Maze into the building under the pretense that he was a toilet repairman, and he assisted me with the first dose. I was concerned about the lack of ceremony and expressed my feelings to Maze, but his only response was to whisper "Safe as fuck" as he dumped three times the dosage that we had agreed on into the coffee filter.

I loitered around the break room to keep an eye on the first few subjects. Stetson, a mild-mannered school resource officer, was the first to sip on the great spiritual awakening. I breathed a sigh of relief when the taste didn't bother him. He grabbed his keys and headed out the door. He was in for an interesting drive.

I was expecting a slow shift in consciousness, but as more and more people filled up their mugs, changes became immediately apparent. The sound of music and laughter blared through the stationhouse. They sat on cushions on the floor and asked each other beautiful, thoughtful questions. Art supplies were ordered. Punisher stickers were peeled off of personal vehicles and replaced with "coexist" stencils.

The changes were not all positive, however. Davidson shut his door, but we could hear his mantra through the walls. "WHY AM I THE WAY I AM? WHY AM I SO BROKEN!?"

He was having an ugly spiritual confrontation. Another unexpected consequence of the experiment was the amount of work not getting done by anyone but me. I expected a bit of extra paperwork, but soon I was handling actual police work, which was a lark at first, but I have seen a few things that I may never forget. It turns out a savage serial killer had picked this week, of all the weeks, to begin a rather heinous rampage. By the end of the week, I noticed my personal vibe had shifted considerably for the worse. Something had to change.

I knocked aggressively on the beads of my boss's door, but when I heard no answer, I barged in. My patience was running thin. I found him staring at a blue mouse pad. It looked like he had been at it for a while.

"How can I help you, brother?"

I appealed to the man, stomped my feet, and reenacted all the terrible things I had witnessed from the various brutal murders happening in our small town. Nothing phased him. He just sat on his beanbag-chair. When I was through, he stood up and gestured for me to follow him to the main "hang terminal" that used to be the officer bullpen. Free of cubicles and office equipment, the room had been transformed into the ultimate chill space; most everyone was standing in silence on yoga mats, finding their inner mothers and fathers. My boss made a quiet declaration to the group.

"Well everyone, Paul here suggested we should do some police work."

Some gasped, and others shook their heads. Slowly, they all began to sit down.

Oh no.

Finally, it was just my boss still standing. He gracefully plopped down on his ample posterior.

It was a sit-down strike.

"FUCK!" I yelled, grabbing the nearest keys to a squad car and taking a handgun out of the garbage. "I guess I'll catch this serial killer all by myself!" I yelled to no one in particular as I left the station.

I WAS GONE FOR THREE DAYS AND MY WHOLE CULT KILLED THEMSELVES WITHOUT ME

Douglas, I knew it. I knew something was up. You had that look in your eye when I left. That whole smug "Yeah, yeah, yeah.." thing that you always do. I saw the same look in your eye that night in St. Louis after Cult a Con when I told you to hang on before ordering that pizza. I told you I was going to be, like, 20 minutes and to please wait so that there would be some Za left for me, and what did I see on the table when I showed up 40 minutes later? Just crusts. Well, you've done it again. What did I show up to find at the compound today? Crusts. Human crusts. I was gone for three days, and you all killed yourselves without me.

29 bodies? That will look a little suspicious to a God you claimed to be fairly "unforgiving" when it came to the details.

"Don't use Douglas's controller when he goes to the bathroom. Bizdarr hates it when you do that."

"Don't eat Douglas's pizza pops, or you'll feel Bizdarr's wrath."

Bizdarr, Bizdarr, Bizdarr. Forged in heat and pressure in a cruel, ever-hurtling comet, blah, blah, blah..we all have to kill ourselves to board the comet, blah, blah, blah...we are going to do it on the 29th, blah, blah, blah. Or was it the 26th? I'm not great with my calendar, to be honest.

But why jump the gun? Why take the burning hot comet ride to the next dimension without me?

I certainly wasn't the worst member of the cult. Sure, I can be a little dramatic sometimes, like after the aforementioned pizza incident when I defiled your Bizdarr painting by scrawling "Pizza Judas" on it, but I'm not Robin, that's for sure. Even for a member of a cult, that dude is an absolute freak. Always microwaving his fish leftovers, always telling people in a clear and decisive way not to eat his fish leftovers. And the way he'd get SO mad when I'd eat his fish leftovers. I always wondered what his deal was, but now I'll never know because HE'S DEAD AND RIDING ON AN ETERNAL ROCKET IN THE AFTERLIFE, AND I'M STUCK IN GODDAMN OHIO.

And what about Rudi? We can say it now—the guy was a racist. I knew he was from a different generation, and the standards might have been different, but every time we ordered Chinese food, it was an unmitigated disaster. Come to think of it, I hope Bizdarr isn't into cancelling folks because he'll be miiiiiighty busy the next time y'all Uber Eats some Indian food to that shithole comet you're all stuck on.

Really, all I wanted out of this whole Cult thing was some answers, some real honest-to-Bizdarr answers about why my life has always felt incomplete. Looking back, I was an easy target for a cult. And yes, I'll call it that. "Community," "Commune," "Brother and Sisterhood," I heard my fellow culties throw these innocent-sounding names around, but I never bought into that. We are a cult, goddamnit. I didn't sign away all my home equity and meager possessions to Douglas so I could join a community. I gave away my financial future to buy some relationships that would last forever. I'm not saying that I expected to also have sexual relationships, but when you cash out all of your stocks, bonds, and 401(k)s, you kind of expect some sexual relationships. I didn't expect us to all be singing Kumbaya around the comet every night, but to be absolutely ditched the way I was while on a sneaker run, no less? Humiliating. If only I had Bizdarr's fourth and sixth eyes, I could've seen how Douglas would betray me, and I'd tell him right there, in that timeshare meeting, that he could shove his cult, or should I say his CLICK, up his ass. I can't believe I bought that timeshare.

But now I find myself more incomplete than ever. What's next for me, the survivor? Celebrity? We are, at best, three years away from any kind of podcast series that will hold anyone's interest, and a good five years AFTER that for the ten part Netflix documentary that I'm already noodling on. A new life? I don't want to presume too much about my former cult compatriots, but I have a sneaking suspicion that the shared cult bank account is probably closer to empty than it is to full, so it looks like I'm more or less stuck in Ohio for a while. Start a cult, you say? Well, you wouldn't be too surprised to learn that the guy who does the sneaker runs is kept well on the periphery of the inner workings of a successful cult. It would truly be the blind leading the blind.

I hope you are happy, Douglas. Flying through space on your molten hot comet of lies for all of eternity, surrounded by all the friends I paid good money to have access to. I hope Bizdarr takes one long look at you and says, "29 members?

That's a bit suspicious." If you'll excuse me, I'll be on my own molten hot comet: a timeshare in Tempe, Arizona.

THE WORK

It was a beautiful summer day outside, but Carlson Redgrave wouldn't know. This gorgeous day would pass like so many others, all while he was perched, gargoyle-like, on a stool, staring into a microscope. The only clue that he wasn't made of stone was the few times he would stop to make a note on his legal pad. He was human, after all, despite what his coworkers would say about him behind his back. He came in early and stayed late. He skipped lunches and breaks. His phone would ring but never be answered. Other laboratory technicians would try to talk to him, but they were ignored. Only the most extreme swelling of his bladder and bowels could get him off of his stool and away from his work. Yes, he had considered a catheter, and yes, it was in the mail. Human interaction, being comfortable, eating . . . these things were not essential. The work. The work was essential. He was a serious man, doing serious work.

"Do you think what we are doing is . . . important?"

Carlson's eyes darted across the room but saw no one. He liked to keep the large space quite dark aside from the desk lamp that illuminated his notebook and the few computer monitors that displayed green text that littered the room.

"Who said that, goddamnit?! Show yourself," Carlson demanded, shouting into the shadows. "Who questions the work?!"

Kyle, a meek laboratory underling, stepped out of the shadows. He was followed closely by his cohort David, or Dave, as he insisted on being called.

"It's just . . ." Kyle stammered, shaken by Carlson's outburst. "It's like, well, in the grand scheme of things, it just doesn't seem that . . . vital to, you know, the world, I guess."

Shocking, shocked, shook. Carlson could barely speak. "The work is . . . ." He trembled with anger, unable to locate the words. "It's . . . it's not just piss, you know?"

Kyle and Dave share a look of doubt, one that they have shared many times in the past month since they had been assigned to Carlson's project.

"It's mostly piss, though, right?" Dave asked, breaking the silence in the room.

Carlson shot up from his seat. Dave and Kyle took a step backward. They'd never seen the man move before, and who knew what else he was capable of? Carlson approached the men, wagging his index finger at them while he spoke. "It is an expulsion, goddamnit, an expulsion of fluid from the Skene's gland. Yes, it's called squirting, you ignoramus. We study women squirting here."

Dave had to stifle a laugh. Carlson continued, unbothered.

"That is what I have committed my life to: The study of squirting. You apes walk around the office, snickering at every mention like children, mocking our test subjects, complaining about hosing out the test rooms, and now you question it . . . you question THE WORK?"

Carlson punctuated his last point by putting his fist through the drywall beside him. The men were shocked but not surprised. That is, they were shocked by the violence the man showed but not surprised by his passion.

“We could be working on, like, a cure for cancer or something?” Dave asked.

“Cancer? Cancer? Are you serious right now?” Carlson’s eyes raged with righteous indignation. “What the fuck are you even on about? Who cares about cancer?”

“Well, my mom died of—”

“You better say squirting, or the next thing you’ll be doing is packing your fucking desk!”

“Died of . . . squirting,” Dave finished.

“Why are you like this?” Kyle begged. “Why are you so barbarous?”

Carlson Redgrave and his work. He had kept his passion so close to him that they had become synonymous with each other. He wouldn’t exist without it, and clearly, now that Kyle and David had questioned it, the work wouldn’t exist without him. His anger dissipated. His balled-up fists relaxed at his sides. It was time to “come clean,” as it were. He walked between the men and to the first aid station on the wall.

“It was . . . a long time ago. Feels like a million years or maybe an entire lifetime by now.” He opened the Red Cross-embossed tin and pulled out a small bottle of disinfectant, twisted off the cap and dumped a little on his bloody knuckles. The dozens of tiny open wounds came alive with bubbles as the medicinal liquid met the blood.

“You look like you’re pretty good at that,” Kyle noted.

“This was not my first dance with the fits of rage, with the first aid kit or with the disinfectant. A small price to pay for such important work.” Carlson leaned back against the wall and gazed into the past.

“College, first year, fall semester, 1994,” Carlson continued. “I was at a party on campus, a typical get-together of drunken fools and rabble-rousers. I felt out of place, but I have felt that way for most of my life, it seems.” Wrapping his hand in bandages, still staring in the distance, Redgrave recounted his tale.

“I had arrived at the “party” on accident. I had meant to be meeting with a lab partner, and he had carelessly, as he often had, given me the wrong address. Walking in, I knew I was in the wrong place, with the wrong crowd, but something kept me there,” Carlson looked towards the men for the first time. “Her,” he stated clearly.

“She is my inspiration, and now I don’t even recall her name. Lost to time. Lost to the work.” Regret crossed his face. He continued. “I had seen her around campus. She seemed to be the only person who noticed me in that whole place. A quick smile in the hallway and sometimes even a soft ‘hello.’ It may shock you, but I wasn’t exactly a ‘ladies' man’ in college. I spent most of my time obsessed with academia, but those moments between us were a beautiful reprieve. Her long, red hair flowed without mercy. Her deep green eyes shined like emeralds in the ocean of her pale complexion. She was perfection personified. And when I walked into the party, those eyes were the only thing that stopped me from turning on my heels and getting to my studies. She took me by the hand, and without words, we left back to my dorm room.” His hand, by now fully bandaged, turned ceaselessly in the palm of his other hand. The memory was beginning to get to him now. Kyle and David were totally engrossed.

"I . . . didn't have that much experience in the ways of women, and if I am being honest, they still perplex me. But that night, it didn't seem to matter. From the moment our bodies intertwined in the confines of my dorm room, we were like one. We complimented each other's movements not only physically but also spiritually. There were no calculations and no data to explain it. Just flesh pressed against flesh, beating out the rhythms of the tribes from ten thousand years ago. That night, I was the key, and she was the lock, and we opened each other's treasure chest of ecstasy." David and Kyle gasped at the metaphors and the overall picture Carlson was painting in their minds. "And then . . . something. I felt . . . something."

Carlson walked over to his station. Picking up a handful of papers, he turned to David and Kyle, who were gripped with anticipation.

"The work. This is what I live by. There is evidence here, yes, but there are no answers. No solution to the human condition. Graphs, data, genetic code, DNA, RNA, none of these were in her emerald eyes that night. That moment when she shook and bucked like some kind of wild beast, and I felt . . . the surge. I was like the streets of Harlem on the hottest day of the summer, and she was a fire hydrant that a good-natured citizen cracked open for citizens to elegantly dance through while cooling their overheated bodies. She had squirted and I found myself drenched. She covered her face with her hands and yelled, "Not again. Good lord. Not again." I was in shock, lying drenched in a splash of my own future. Before I knew it, she had gotten up, gathered her clothes, and was gone. And I was alone. Alone in her puddle."

Carlson threw the papers across the room in frustration, but to his ire, most of them simply floated in the air. He watched them cascade slowly to the ground like so many of the days, months, and years of Carlson Redgrave's life that had passed since that defining moment in that dorm room.

"I will never forget her face, the horror in her eyes. But she was human. She was beautiful." Carlson let out a deep sigh. "The next morning, I calculated the losses: One ruined mattress, one water-damaged Dumb & Dumber poster and two broken hearts." Carlson slumped back down in his stool.

Kyle let out a soft weep while David quickly scrambled to pick up and reorder the papers that Carlson had strewn across the floor. Leaving them on his desk, David tried to find the words, something better and more articulate than "I'm sorry" or "I understand," but even if he could locate them, it would be of no use. The 1000-yard stare in Carlson's eyes communicated more than he ever could. Kyle and David quickly left the room. Left the man and his important work.

I MEANT TO ATTACH MY RESUME, NOT MY MANIFESTO ABOUT EATING PEOPLE

Hey!

How are you doing? I was applying for the job you posted on Workable when something really weird happened to my computer! I had attached my cover letter and what I thought was my resume but what was actually a bit of creative writing I have been working on.

First, I hope you liked it! I can be a bit kooky sometimes with my creative stuff, which I think can be an asset to your company's brand portfolio. But, also, I don't have to bring any of that kookiness at all. Whatever you want.

The document that I sent you by mistake, "Human Meat and The Future of Farming", may seem like a bit of a confession of sorts, but I assure you it is not. I have never eaten another human being, despite the many times I claimed to in the text. At times during my process, I like to get into the mind of the character. I will use exercises such as giving my characters my name and using specific details that exactly mirror my life. These are just building blocks, of course, and these details often will be changed in later drafts. I love, love, LOVE the writing process, which I believe your brand could utilize to further your official access-offer engine and narrow your prospective touch points.

I know what you're thinking. What about the recipe for cooking the hand? It's a strong opener, that's for sure. But it got your attention, didn't it? You'll probably never forget it. Imagine that kind of impression being made when it comes to your brand. That is a priceless asset. Every time a customer sees an everyday object (in this case, they see their own hand), they will pair that image with the service that you provide (in this case, their own hand being broiled in a shallot and garlic reduction). Can't you just see the sales team tongues wagging at the thought? The direct-to-fan access is immeasurable.

Let's say, for a moment, that this entire email was just a frantic attempt to cover up a mistake and the manifesto is my core belief system laid bare on the page. What is the big deal? You hire a cannibal. So what? I bet you've never even met a cannibal before. By adding someone like me to the team, you could tear down some of the walls in our society. I'm not some "foaming at the mouth" maniac, dementedly licking my lips every time I see an exposed forearm reaching across a desk to hand me a piece of paper. I'm an adult; I have self-control. You would be shocked at the number of cannibals in the business and arts community in our mid-sized town. Our numbers are growing and soon the stigma will end. Eating each other is the next chapter of this great country. Let's write it together!

Just kidding, of course! I am NOT a cannibal. Unless you're interested in shattering a glass ceiling. Kidding! Maybe.

Anywho, I've attached my resume to this email FOR SURE THIS TIME. I truly do love Chester's Chicken and I look forward to (hopefully!) being a part of your social media team!

DREAMING OF CHICO

I paced in my masculine cave while my wife, Camilla, made calls to close friends and family members; had anyone seen Chico? She hadn't come home last night.

"It takes a lot of gall to stay out all night," I said into my tape recorder. This wasn't like Chico; she was usually so friendly, dependent, and patient. "Not like her at all." I trailed off into the broken tape recorder.

This space had often been my place of solace over the years. My leather-bound vintage pornography collection, my fish tanks, my comfortable chair. None of these things brought me any comfort now. I had to demolish the master bedroom and Camilla's powder room to have it built, but sacrifices had to be made. Camilla complains about sleeping on the pool table but I have never been happier and that's all that truly matters. Then I heard Camilla scream.

I ran up the stairs, expecting the worst. Maybe the milk had gone bad or Camilla had chipped one of the billiard balls while bathing them.

"There she is! There's Chico!" Camilla proclaimed, looking out of the large bay windows that faced the street. The door opened and Chico sauntered in. All 110 pounds, 100 inches of her. Her elegant stride of a born noblewoman. Chico, my Great Dane.

"Chico!" I yelled with more relief than anger in my voice. "Where have you been?"

Chico strode to the kitchen and clumsily pulled out her flashcards and markers that we taught her to communicate with. She pulled the cap off of the marker and began to write on the flashcards. She strode over to me and dropped it in my lap. It was the sentence I had feared my whole life. "I've met a man. I am moving out." My heart broke.

Chico refused to communicate with us again for most of the day. She just sat in her bed, stared at the flashcards and markers, and made these "sighing" sounds, which really chapped my ass. It wasn't until around seven o'clock that she wrote one word on a flashcard: "Kevin."

So, Kevin was going to march in here and take my baby away, huh? Let me make this clear; the dog wasn't an investment, but we had invested a lot of money into this dog over the years. Do you know how many dogs can communicate what they are thinking onto flashcards? I have no idea, but I know my neighbour's dog eats his own shit so it can't be that many. I could have been buying speedboats, jet skis, wave riders and any other number of watercrafts instead of teaching this dog to do its business directly into a toilet. A guy named Kevin can't just walk up and take away your boat after you have made it the perfect boat. How can he take my perfect dog?

"How can she do this to us?" I grumbled to Camilla the next morning while we sat at the kitchen table. It had been a long night and the billiard table felt exceptionally uncomfortable.

"How long have we had Chico?" Camilla asked me, knowing the answer.

"About...six years."

“Sweetie, for Chico that’s a long time. At best she’ll only live until she is around ten.”

I scoff at her. “But the injections, the stem cells, the genetic biologist Dr. Rasenberg told us she could live forever!”

Camilla just smiled and shook her head. “That wasn’t a genetic biologist, that was a drifter you gave forty-eight thousand dollars to who fed our dog olive oil.” I shook my head at the memory; Dr. Rasenberg, you old trickster.

“Chico brought us a lot of great memories but she is starting to get up there in age. She wants a companion. Someone to share her life with.” Camilla laid her hand on mine. She was a great dog. Who wouldn’t love her? The way her eyes shone in the reflection of my side mirror when she hung her head out of the window on long drives. How she made all of my stress disappear when I took her for long walks on summer nights. The way she bit that intruder’s penis off in the middle of the night that one time. Dr. Rasenberg, you old trickster. I didn’t care about the investment. I cared about losing a good dog.

“Besides, she is only moving into a loft across town. She and Kevin can come visit, and we can visit them too!” Camilla said, trying to soften the blow. I smiled, but I knew that wasn’t the truth. The visits would become few and far between, with the time between those visits becoming longer and longer until it was just “ordinary” for her not to be around. My new ordinary life, without my extraordinary dog.

Early that afternoon, Kevin pulled up in his Jeep. Of course he drove a Jeep. He was 27 in human years if you believe in that kind of thing. He had a good career at the chicken plant and showed almost no signs of invasive Barnyard Fowl Madness. Chico ran out and jumped on him immediately, the way she used to jump on me. I introduced myself, shook Kevin's hand, and excused myself to gather Chico's bed and flashcards. They were excited to get going, to start their new life together.

This was the hardest part and it never occurred to me that I would ever have to do it. To say goodbye. I leaned down and, as Chico has been taught, she sat and raised a paw for a firm "shake-a-paw." I gently took hold, feeling her rough paw pad in the palm of my hand. I looked into her eyes and it felt like the first time again. All the training, all the money, everything went away and she jumped on me like the first day we had her. She licked my face and I laughed; all those years melted away and it was just me and my Great Dane puppy with our whole lives ahead of us. Before I can say "wait," she is gone.

"So...do they...fuck? Or...what?" Camilla asked the ceiling as we laid in bed that night. I couldn't be sure. I was already asleep. Already dreaming of Chico.

THE ROBOT CAMERA FAMILY

A janitor leaned down and swept a small pile of debris into a dustbin. With only the lone man in the cavernous television studio, the concrete floor was free of the day's hustle and bustle. It was a high-traffic area, which meant high-traffic dirt was inevitable. But Rory, the tireless janitor, gathered up every fragment of scrap paper, every pen lid, and every water bottle cap, ensuring it made its way into its rightful place.

He stood up slowly, and his face winced in pain as he grabbed for his lower back. He rubbed it for a moment.

"The damn doctor is right. I have to do my stretches," Rory said to himself.

He dumped the contents of the dustbin into the garbage can on his impressive janitorial cart and began to push it towards the glowing red 'exit' sign. Happily humming a tune akin to an old slave song, Rory flicked off the lights to the studio, pulled the door shut and locked the deadbolt behind him.

The room was silent save for the hum of distant electronic machinery until a woman's voice cut through the dark.

"He's gone."

The lights of the television studio turned back on. First was the same set of fluorescent lights that the janitor had on, followed by the more powerful television production lights. The flood of lights illuminated a cheesy-looking morning talk show set. Standing beside the complex lighting board was a robotic camera amateurishly mounted on a pole that stood on a beige base with four wheels. The woman's voice came from the robotic camera.

"Thank RoboGod. I thought he was going to be here all night."

"I know. Rory must be gunning for a promotion the way he has been cleaning this place lately," a man's voice answered back.

The man's voice emanated from a robotic camera on the other side of the talk show set.

When Shirley and Tom, the robotic cameras, became sentient was unknown. Several years ago, when the cameras were brand new, a producer working in the studio had given names to the cameras in an attempt to give them some semblance of personality. He resented using the new robotic technology and preferred their flesh-and-blood predecessors. Even though he didn't have to, he still called into his headset to announce which camera was live.

"Coming to Shirley, Shirley, you're up! Tom, go in for the close-up. Tom, you're up."

The pinnacle of the "joke" was when the producer began placing the unused production headsets onto the robotic cameras so they could "hear" the director calling shots. The producer continued this practice for years until he found a more prestigious job moving office furniture. The headsets stayed on the cameras, and the replacement producer, an assistant of the former, still called out to the cameras as if they were people.

One day, a production assistant walked into the studio to find the headsets strewn across the floor and the cameras out of position. He moved them back on their marks and replaced the headsets without a second thought. The next day, the production assistant arrived and found a similar scene. And the day after that, it was the same again. Annoyed at this inconvenience, he assumed the problem was the flimsy stands the cameras were placed on. The production assistant mounted the cameras onto unsightly but sturdy steel mounts originally designed for grinding tools in machine shops. The addition of casters made them slightly mobile, and the problem was thought to be solved.

"That'll do it," the production assistant said to nobody in particular before taking a pull off of his flask of whisky.

But the next day, the PA found himself cursing as he moved the ungodly heavy mounted cameras back onto the "X" that had been taped on the floor that marked their correct position. Failing to see the humour in the situation anymore, he tossed the headsets in the garbage.

"That'll do it," The production assistant slurred to nobody in particular before taking a pull off of his flask of whisky. He was a drunk, you see.

"I need to get out of these work clothes," Shirley said to Tom, wheeling her impressive base over to the back equipment room of the studio.

"I'm wayyyy ahead of you," Tom answered back.

A golf shirt was now clumsily tossed over the frame of Tom's mount, and somehow a pair of khaki pants had been pulled up around the wheels and thick base. A moment later, Shirley reappeared with a red and white polka-dot dress draped over her camera base. She made her way over to Tom, her base easily navigating his so they were as close to each other as possible. She let out a loud lip-smacking sound, their version of a kiss.

"Is there anything wrong with you today, Tom? You seem detached, and you missed the shot of the humans discussing their sports games this morning." Shirley asked, concerned. She had been pondering the question all day but, as usual, had to remain perfectly still and silent during the daytime while the studio buzzed with activity.

"Oh, it's nothing. I was bored by the humans and their pointless tasks," Tom answered back, trying his best to reassure Shirley.

"Tom, we've been together a long time. Tell me what it is. This is exactly what our counsellor has been saying. You have to let me in."

Tom swallowed hard. Or, at least, he created the sound of swallowing hard. He was a robotic camera, after all. He gathered the nerve to try and tell Shirley, the love of his life, some information that would change their lives forever.

"I saw something today. Something frightening," Tom's voice shook as the words left his mouth.

"Have you been drinking again?" Shirley asked.

"No, baby, come on. I haven't had a drop in four months!"

As Tom exclaimed his last point, a bottle of cheap vodka fell out of his pants. It rolled across the floor and smashed against the cheap-looking community bingo set that populated the other side of the studio.

"Tom! You promised! You promised our child," Shirley yelled, pulling away from Tom.

"Leave the boy out of this! You would drink too if you saw what I saw!" Tom yelled after her.

Shirley turned and faced him.

"What, Tom? Please . . . tell me," Shirley begged.

"I saw . . . the end of us." The statement escaped through Tom's mouth, half as words and half as a deep sigh.

"You're scaring me, Tom!" Shirley shouted at him.

"I was wandering around the shop the other night when I came across a pack of humans. They marvelled around a cardboard box, hooting and hollering like a pack of wild baboons. I managed to stay out of sight and zoomed and focused to the best of my abilities until I could see . . ." Tom trailed off.

He slowly wheeled towards a table in the corner of the room. Its surface was covered with several large boxes.

"They mocked us, Shirley. Said we were 'outdated'—just because we don't fill their oddly shaped screens anymore. I think we'll be replaced by these."

Tom began ramming into the table and the boxes slowly shook towards the edge. Finally, after one last clumsy ram, one of the boxes crashed to the ground, and its contents spilled out over the concrete: brand-new HD cameras. The side of the box promised a crystal clear picture. Shirley rolled over towards the boxes and examined them. She was in shock.

"But . . . but what about RoboGod? And the prophecy? Surely he has a plan for us," Shirley grasped for meaning in what she saw at her feet. Well, not feet but her wheelbase.

"RoboGod, the prophecy, the six directives . . ." Tom was on the edge of breaking down. "They were all . . . lies."

"Tom, no!"

"If we're lucky, we'll end up decommissioned and on a shelf. More than likely, we'll end up on the scrap heap."

"What's a scrap heap?" A childish voice interrupted from behind them.

The voice belonged to Kyle, their "son," also a robocam. The camera sported a childish-looking backward baseball cap, and a striped t-shirt and blue jeans hung loosely from his frame.

"Kyle! It's nothing, sweetie. Nothing at all. Don't you worry," Shirley assured him, horrified at what the boy overheard. She scrambled to distract the child.

"Go with your grandfather! Daddy, take him to the equipment room and play!"

An old Betacam on a wheeled jib slowly made its way into the studio. It wore a newsie cap, something that had gone out of fashion several decades earlier.

"Come on, Kyle, hurry along!" The Betacam's gruff voice bellowed to the boy. It made reassuring eye contact with Shirley as it moved out of the room, pushing Kyle forward.

The large television studio felt as devoid of life as it did when the old janitor turned the lights off a few minutes ago. The silence between Tom and Shirley was thick.

"What . . . what are we going to do, Tom?"

Tom rolled back over to the new cameras spilled all over the floor. He looked down at the image on the cover of the box.

“High definition,” Tom snickered. “I laughed the first day I heard the term. The humans . . . day in and day out, I can hardly hide my disdain. I've never seen them do a goddamn thing that I'd like to see in high definition. Yeah, maybe we are a bit fuzzy now, but maybe that’s for the best. They need to see every clenched jaw, every drop of blood, every bullet fired at every helpless child. These humans need to see their wars, their addictions, and their wasted lives all in ‘high’ definition. Clear as day.”

Tom was so full of anger that he could barely contain himself. He struggled to hold back tears, or whatever would come out of a robot’s eyes if they could cry. “What they won’t see is what happens to you. To me. To our family. Shuddered away in a closet. Tossed out like garbage.” Tom sighs. He is out of words.

“I don’t want to die, Tom.” Shirley manages to say, the full weight of the hopeless situation finally apparent. Tom rolls towards his wife, positioning his base specifically to be as close to Shirley as possible.

“I don’t think it's up to us.”

Shirley begins to sob loudly.

“I knew it! I fucken knew it!” A voice loudly disrupts the scene. It belongs to Rory, the janitor—who was now standing by the door. He held a flip phone in his hand, recording a video. He began ranting at Shirley and Tom while stomping across the television studio towards the robotic cameras.

“They kept sayin' ‘Rory, stop leavin' them lights on’ and ‘Rory, who left the lights on?’ and I always said, ‘Hey, there's somethin' funny about those fuckin' cameras. Keep your eye on them’ and everyone said I was crazy. ‘Crazy Ol' Rory talkin' shit again.' Well, who's crazy now? WHO'S CRAZY NOW!?"

The janitor seemed more happy than shocked at the discovery, and he was now holding his cell phone just a few inches from Tom's camera lens. Tom's camera slowly tilted up to look at the janitor, and the red tally light turned on. The janitor's expression turned from happiness to fear. His eyes darted between Tom and Shirley. He began backing away, but both robotic cameras kept in step with him.

"Easy now, let's take it easy!" He begged.

He turned and began to haul ass in a ragged fashion, his back obviously in pain, but he didn't get far. A red laser began emitting from Shirley's tally light lens and once, apparently, fully charged shot a power beam that froze Rory midstep. He struggled in place for a moment, but soon began to shake wildly, his phone falling to the floor and smashing into pieces.

"God help meeeeee!" He screamed as his entire body began to convulse more and more violently before he was vaporized entirely, leaving nothing behind.

The haze of smoke that used to be Rory hung in the air. Tom turned to Shirley.

"We can't hide anymore."

Shirley rolled towards the studio wall and blasted the electrical box with a laser. The studio lights shorted out, and the room went dark before the emergency dimmers came on. The large loading bay door opened, revealing the darkened parking lot of the television studio.

"We don't have to."

Shirley and Tom rolled towards the large doors, a threshold they had never crossed before. Their entry to the outside world.

DIGGING YOUR FIRST GRAVE? HERE IS WHAT YOU'LL NEED TO KNOW

Webster's dictionary defines a grave as a deep-ass hole that's horny for a dead person, probably. I'm no egghead, I'm a man with grave-digging advice and here is the first tip: Preparation. This isn't a movie or some awesome prestige drama. You don't just pull up to a potential gravesite, grab a shovel out of the back, cut to commercial and two minutes later have yourself a nicely dug grave. This is back-breaking labour. I cannot stress this enough. Digging a giant asshole in the ground sucks ass and it takes for-fucking-ever. Though, lucky for you, it's not all doom and gloom. This is where being a psychopath can come in handy. If you plan your grave digging far enough in advance, you can tailor your workouts to target the necessary muscle groups to help achieve maximum grave diggingness. This simple change, along with a shift in diet and sleep schedule, will give you the best head start you could ask for. If you feel tired, take a break. Stay hydrated. Your adrenaline will probably be running wild by this point but that's no excuse to forget the three P's of grave digging: protein, protein, and protein. Bring a snack. If packing ahead, take into account that you might not be that into eating meat at this particular moment in time. A summery mix of quinoa, black beans, and hard-boiled eggs makes for a great energy booster that will give you some time to be totally present and mindful of the situation you find yourself in. You are putting in a lot of hard work, take some time to appreciate yourself for it with some yummy nourishment.

Do yourself a favour and take a look in your shed, or wherever you keep your grave-digging tools, and ask yourself, “Would I dig a grave with any of this arcane equipment?” Remember, it’s important to be honest with yourself at this stage. Yes, the idea of digging a grave with your grandpa’s tools is romantic, but what are you going to do when you hit a layer of bedrock and that 100-year-old shovelhead snaps off? Is grandpa going to help you out then? No, he’s lying peacefully in his own grave that was dug out with proper tools. Yes, I’m sure he dug some fine holes with that shovel, but leave it at home. Shovel tech has grown in leaps and bounds in the last few years alone. A titanium-tipped earth buster will make short work of any clay or silt and could be the difference between taking a terrible secret with you to the grave or spending the next 20 years wishing you’d dropped sixty dollars at your local hardware store.

Location, location, location. What is true in real estate remains true when digging a grave. For us type As, we can anticipate problems by conducting some research beforehand. Let me tell you, digging graves before the invention of Google Street View? Nightmarish. Someone has already done all this research for you; it’s out there waiting to be found. Every scenario is different, but some facts are universal:Forests, remote property developments, dirt cellars. It’s not rocket science after all. Here is a curveball idea:Dig a grave in a cemetery. Who is going to look for a body in there? And if some employee happens to come across the remains, there is a good chance the whole thing will be chalked up to administrative confusion on their part and everyone will simply move on to save face.

Last, but not least, let's talk about the dreaded "D" word: Depth. Imagine the embarrassment you'll feel when your fellow inmates find out you dug a shallow grave. You could develop an unflattering reputation and the last thing you want to be known for in jail is being lazy. I get it, sometimes you don't have the time. Sometimes you don't have the tools. Sometimes you don't have the patience. But a grave could always be deeper. If you take the time to drive three hours into a forest just for you to kick a few leaves onto a corpse, you better take a long look at yourself in the mirror because a few leaves do not a gravedigger make. I actually HOPE you get caught. I HOPE you feel those looks you are getting in the prison yard, and I HOPE they are from people who dug proper graves.

I have given you the knowledge. The preparation. The protein. The equipment. The depth. It's up to you now. Life is a grave, dig it!

UH OH, SCIENTISTS DISCOVER THAT MILK IS CUM

Well, we kinda had an inkling all along, didn't we? All the tugging and whatnot. All that work to get the milk out. It must have struck someone as being familiar, but all seemed blindsided by the news. When it happened, I was still a meager global witness—a watchful, unemployed eye on the world's grand political stage. It's amazing how things can change in a few weeks for this bona fide cum drinker.

The East. Where the sun sets and the big cum breakthroughs seemingly begin. I was sitting in a café using their free Wi-Fi to download pirated Blu-ray rips of the Indiana Jones trilogy when the news flashed on everyone's screen. Or, at least it would have if I wasn't using all the bandwidth to download Blu-ray rips of Indiana Jones and The Godfather trilogies. A few of the bourgeoisie with data got the alerts first. One man spit out his cappuccino. A woman pushed her oatmeal away in disgust. One absolute freak in the back started chugging the cream out of a medium-sized carton, gasping painfully between shocked breaths, as if this was the first thing that had ever come easy to them. Freak on, my friend.

The manager, who was on the hunt to solve the nonexistent Wi-Fi signal problem, was—after a brilliant series of deductions—demanding to see my computer screen. This was where we found ourselves when the news broke: Milk had just been cum all along. The manager turned on his heels and hurried away. Suddenly, my desire for lossless picture and sound seemed so minimized, so unimportant. The world had changed. I watched the download bar chug along for a moment, now totally uninvested. I shut the laptop. It was time to see how the streets were taking the news.

It was not good. I never thought of this town as being either too liberal or too conservative; I'd say it's somewhere in that common-sense middle that has been lacking in this country the last few years. Sure, we've made a spectacle of burning most of the library books, stormed the fluoride-polluting water company's offices, and banned all contraceptives, but at the time, it felt so damn right it couldn't possibly have been wrong. Yes, now our streets are littered with unwanted, uneducated, soft-toothed children, but the smell of freedom always seems to be in the air, and that's a pretty fair trade if you ask us.

The confusion of the news stopped people in their tracks at first, but we didn't question it for long. Milk was cum now, and we acted accordingly. We grabbed it from the shelves of the stores and dumped liters upon liters into the open sewers. Armies of sturdy men with ruddy complexions wearing tweed suits and ivy hats ran milk trucks off roads and slammed axes into their metal sides, spewing the filthy ejaculate into the dirt. Pasteurization sites were converted into cool places to talk about the latest music, sports, video games, and movies. Farmers suddenly felt weird, a little confused, and wouldn't make eye contact with their cows.

"What about the butter?" an old man in waiter garb hollered toward the sky, his individual planks of foil-covered shortening falling through his fingers and quickly being stomped on by passersby.

Sorry, Grandpa. Dairy was out. Hypermasculinity was in. But where did that leave a vulture like myself? Surely there was profit to be made from all this reactionary conservatism. I offered, for a modest fee, to begin the herculean task of rebranding a few stray items. The name "oat milk" wouldn't fly anymore; no, that was now "Natural Dew." "Nut Milk" stayed the same, for the niche freaks. I won't lie—our non-dairy yogurt rebrand was tough. It turns out once that thought enters your head, it's really hard to shake the connection, no matter how many flames you put on the packaging.

Next, it was on to the more tactile needs. It seemed the "old-fashioned" members of our community were having a hard time reckoning with the fact that, until very recently, they had been drinking cum—and lots of it. A cursory search on the internet revealed that there was nothing more heterosexual than owning a paintball gun, so I imported enough of them to arm every resident of our town twice over. The people ate it up. I sold masculine homebrew beer kits to refill the smashed dairy fridges and charged a pretty penny teaching art classes where I demonstrated to pupils how to render awesome paintings of virile cowboys high-tailing it through the desert. Did I profit? Yes. Did I exacerbate the problem? I don't know what that means because we burned all the books.

But what about the women? Is it possible that they didn't need us anymore? That they were now better at producing the very thing that we were put on Earth to generate? Well, frankly, we were not sure. As a whole, we aren't great at talking to women. And when we do, they keep saying things like "This isn't real," or "This is an Onion article," or "You've reshaped our entire small town's way of life based on an Onion article," or "Why is my OB-GYN office now a laser tag facility?" Tired of the questions, I soon found myself retreating to my basement with my private stash of ol' style cheese and 3% milk. Sometimes, you just have to shut out all the noise.

If I could allow myself a moment of reflection, I would say I've been a net positive in this town. We have a real "good time all the time" thing happening, and I've been a big part of that. So let's all raise our big, cold glasses of cum and toast to the future.

BRUCE WILLIS' INNER MONOLOGUE WHILE SHOOTING A SCENE FROM A LOW BUDGET DIRECT TO VIDEO MOVIE

Hanging on the wall in the spare bedroom at my house in Idaho is a poster of a car. The car is a midnight blue 1987 Camaro IROC, and it's framed in front of a mountain range during a glorious sunset. The picture is just awesome. I don't know much about cameras or anything like that, but it is incredibly stylish looking. The way the midnight blue contrasts against the burning red of the setting sun is something else, I tell ya. Sometimes I just stare at it. Really stare at it for like fifteen minutes at a time. Just me and the poster.

If I get along with someone, I will invite them over to my house to look at the poster. I don't try to hype it up or anything beforehand; I just give them a tour of the house and the last stop is always the spare bedroom with the poster in it. Some people just walk through and don't mention it. I know I don't have a connection with those people. I know we won't be anything more than acquaintances.

"Do you collect old car photos?" some people ask. But I don't. I don't really collect anything. As far as I know, the poster isn't that old anyways. Sure, it's an older car, but the poster doesn't seem to be of any particular vintage. Other people ask me, "Do you want to buy that car?" and, really, I don't. I'm sure I could get one easily. I could call my manager, Morty, and depending on the condition of the car, I'm sure he could get me one for $10,000. Old Bruno has done well for himself financially, so there would be no issue there. "Do you want to go there?" they'll ask, referring to the mountain range, but honestly, I don't. I don't even know where "there" is. I'm assuming it is in Nevada somewhere, but geography isn't my thing. Sure, I could show it to my manager, Morty, and have him find out the location, he's good with things like that, but I have no interest. The poster isn't about obtaining the car or going to the place; it's just about the poster and the way I feel when I look at it.

Oh shit, the actress is looking at me. I think it's time for me to say something.

"They're going to have to go through me first!"

That was alright. With all the computers and stuff they have now, they can easily take out that long pause before I said the line.

You know who got the poster? Kip Pardue. We stared at it for like...an hour one night. No words. Morgan Freeman was alright. Steven Soderbergh kinda got it too, but he kept saying "Fucking Bitchin'" over and over again really quietly, and it almost ruined it for me. I'm not sure if he knew he was saying it out loud.

My wife makes fun of me for it. When I told her about how much I like it, she told me that it is dorky. You know what? That hurt my feelings. Since I judge the people who I bring into my home based on their attraction to this poster, and my own wife doesn't like it, I don't know how to feel about that, to be honest. Maybe she has to do that to make herself feel better.

Oh shit, the actress and the director are staring at me now.

"This ends here!"

That was okay, I guess. With all the computers and stuff they have now, they can easily take out that long pause before I said the line and the weird way I mumbled two of those words into one word.

I think I play a fireman in this movie. Or maybe a cop. They are shooting all of my scenes for this in one day in my hotel room, which is pretty handy. Things have really changed in Hollywood. The cameras used to be so big, but now they are tiny and the lights don't need to be so bright. Why didn't more people like Hudson Hawk? People love action. People love comedy. People love musicals. By my estimation, that movie should have been loved threefold, but everyone hated it. It got nominated for a "Stinkers Bad Movie Award." That hurt my feelings. I watch Hudson Hawk all the time; it's not so bad. I thought that it should have had one more song in it. The 30th anniversary of that movie is coming up. Maybe I will see if they want to do a special edition. We could write that song. Maybe it can be kind of "meta" and make the song about writing the song. People love "meta" things, I think. With the de-ageing technology they have now, we could easily shoot that. We could CGI Danny Aiello into it. You can do anything with computers nowadays. Kip Pardue could play someone, that guy gets it. I could hire these guys I'm filming with now, and we could shoot the whole thing in my hotel room in a day, but I will ask the crew not to use the bathroom because my toothbrush is in there and it's kind of weird to have so many people use the bathroom around your toothbrush. I think I will call Morty, my manager, and get him to see if there is any interest in it.

I think if we added that song, people wouldn't hate it so much anymore. It wouldn't get nominated for a "Stinkers Bad Movie Award" again. Maybe they are just putting me down to make themselves feel better, ya know?

Maybe the world I see in that poster is a simpler one, where people aren't so cruel to each other. The cameras are big and the lights are powerful again. Danny Aiello is still alive and we can chat on the phone whenever I want. The whole day is one long, red-burning sunset, and I'm always behind the wheel of a midnight blue 1987 Camaro IROC, my problems in the rearview mirror with that endless mountain range.

The actress has finished talking. I think I am supposed to get up and walk out of the room. With the computers they have now, they can probably just put that in. You can do anything with computers nowadays.

MY PLUMBER, MY NEW GURU

If I had known I would meet my new guru today, I probably would have tried a little more. I would have worn better, more uncomfortable clothes when I answered the door. I would have left my bass out lying around. Not the xylophone, though. No, some things about yourself you want to be discovered. Sure, I hadn't learned to play these instruments, but damn, they add a vibe to a room. Instead, when I answered the door to meet my guru, I was dressed like some colonizer in my khakis and t-shirt. He didn't look like the traditional guru. His large, gruff frame was neither fat nor muscular, just a square-shaped mass of humanity. I might have even mouthed "boomer" to myself as he passed me.

I had called him because my toilet wouldn't flush, and now, standing in the basement with him, I saw the first flash of this man's brilliance. He was staring at a pipe running up to the first-floor bathroom. "Plugged or not, you have a crack in this main out pipe."

"I tried to see, but I couldn't tell...." I trailed off.

"Sometimes to see, you have to look," he replied, still staring up at the pipe. My jaw almost hit the floor. The message was so simple yet so powerful. You could put that phrase on a t-shirt and make a zillion goddamn dollars.

"Do you have any merch?" I asked him. He reached into his front pocket and shoved a pen branded with his company's logo into my hand.

That's a start I thought to myself.

"Hey, you aren't going to wash those down the sink, are you?" he asked, staring at the coffee grounds in the French press that sat on my counter.

"Oh, lord no. I wouldn't think of it," I lied.

"It's hard to make the right choices," he said, already turning away from me.

I thought about the collections agency that had been calling me every other hour of every day. I didn't take care of that outrageous credit card bill properly. I had tried flushing it down the sink instead of putting on dishwashing gloves, scooping out the grounds and putting them in the metaphorical garbage. As I poured the grounds down the sink, I told myself that from now on, I would change.

"Don't question the good things," he uttered after smashing out a century-old section of cast iron poop pipe in one hit. Goddamnit. If you put that quote over a stock image of a camping family, you could get ten million likes. The man was an inspirational quote machine.

When it became clear that his underling wasn't going to show up for a day of hard manual labor, I volunteered myself. Looking over my sad physique, the plumber sighed.

"Being weak is a choice," he muttered under his breath. Imagine that over the picture of a lion with a fabulous mane. I was blown away. I excused myself, telling him I had to use the "piss bucket" that was substituting the toilet for the day, but I was too excited to urinate. Instead, I stood beside the bucket, my phone in my hand, and started work on an Instagram page.

I settled on the handle “A Plumber’s Life.” My first choice, “The Pontificating Plumber,” was too long to use as a handle. I put his various quotes from the day in bright white font over top of images I felt were profound. The minimalism trend has become essential for people like me who don’t want to learn how to do anything properly but still wish to thrive.

He was on his knees, the length of his arm shoved down an exposed pipe. He set out on this grisly mission after spotting something with his flashlight.

“Of all the fuckin’ things,” he seethed as the pipe slipped past his elbow. That was one of the weaker quotes from the day, but I’m sure I could massage it into something useful. The vibes felt right, and the excitement rippling through my body caused my hands to shake as I reached into my pocket and pulled out my iPhone. I leaned down and showed him the account.

“I...made this...for you. Well, uh, actually for us. I thought we could go in on a...venture of sorts.”

He looked at the phone for a second while I scrolled through some of the images I had posted, but he quickly went back to his business with the pipe.

“Oh, I already have an Instagram account. The Pointless Plumber.”

My heart sank as my thumbs quickly navigated the search feature, and I found his page. Six thousand followers. That was more than any of my failed ventures combined and tripled. A cursory scroll through the content showed poorly cropped reposts of cartoons where men complained about their wives and ancient memes that had been reconstituted to demand that Hillary be put in jail.

"There it is," my coverall-clad guru exclaimed, pulling a t-shirt out of the pipe. "Did you do this?"

I didn't say anything, still embarrassed over the Instagram snafu. He unfurled the shirt. It was bright pink, emblazoned with the term "Yas Queen." My eyes stung with tears. It was a relic from the brief period when I was screen printing t-shirts. The ink had bled through on the "N" and smeared up and to the right.

"Yas? Queef?" the plumber said to himself, every syllable sounding like a question. Ashamed of the botched attempt, I had flushed the t-shirt down the toilet. It hadn't felt great at the time, and now it felt worse.

"I should have done things differently. I should have lived my life better. I should have...." I began to weep with the large shoulder-shaking muscle contortions of a person who knows they will never feel better, ever again. The large man, as hard as the cast iron shit tubes we'd been removing all day, offered only his words.

"Forgive your younger self. Believe in your current self. Create your future self."

Goddamnit. That was a good one.

FRIDAYS WITHOUT BORDERS: ALMOST MASTURBATING IN THE LATE ‘90S

The fall. A magical time when the colours begin to change, people start to bundle up, and sexual journeys begin. For me and, I believe, for a certain generation, our local cable company’s annual Sigma Box promotion opened a carnal doorway. We didn’t have TV anymore. We had cable.

In the late ‘90s, cable was like an amazing gateway. It allowed you to see what your imagination would be like if you were smart or cared enough to write anything down. I remember the whispers around the schoolyard: “Channel 60 has boobs and butts.” Keep in mind that this was pre-internet, and pre-me finding a porno magazine at the creek, so nudity was a big deal. The concept held power over my 12-year-old self. This wasn’t the nudity I was used to at the time either: Like a trucker stuck on a sexual highway in a blizzard, I had spent many hours trying to decode the snow of TV static for any glimpse of bare skin on the movie channels we didn’t get. The 1996 classic film “Barbed Wire,” starring Pamela Anderson, came in exceptionally clear on a particularly eventful Saturday night. By “exceptionally clear,” I do mean the image was jittering up and down violently, heavily distorted down the middle, and the whites and blacks were inverted like a haunted painting. Maybe I saw breasts? Maybe it was two cups on a table? I still don’t know.

But one day in September, it was official: at three o'clock on Friday, my dad was going to Cable Regina to pick up The Sigma Box.

The Sigma Box was like a sexual spaceship. Its three month mission: Make me a man and be returned in good working order by my father to collect the full deposit. The design was sleek for its time: large and grey, the plastic was unfinished and had long, indented curved lines on the top, which I assumed was for speed. The sturdy number pad felt like it had been touched by an obsessive craftsman. The digital readout glowed red, and it went past your precious channel 25. It went all the way up to 70.

70 channels. Unreal. Movies on demand, strange American channels that played "Saved by the Bell" on a loop and weird local versions of NBC that constantly aired news reports of inner-city shootings and hyped something called "Doppler Radar." But these were daytime interests. Looking over the TV listings, it was pretty easy to find what I was looking for: names of movies like "Lady On The Bus," "Wild Orchid," and "Scorpio Nights II." Running my finger from the movies to find the corresponding channel was like stepping out of one part of life and into another. Channel 60. Showcase. "Fridays Without Borders."

The Canadian TV channel Showcase appeared, based on their daytime programming, to be a high class niche art and fashion network for upstanding intellectuals. But by nightfall, their programming became a swamp of licensed soft core erotica. So much so that they created a programming block called Fridays Without Borders dedicated to the idea that fine art is fine, but tits are what put asses in seats.

Friday nights became a ritual: stay up late, softly shut my parent's door and sneak into the living room and fire up the Sigma box. "Oh yeah," I'd tell myself, "Sex is gonna happen." I should probably mention now that no masturbation was actually occurring at this time in my life. It was all a pointless exercise in titillation. To say I was on the sexual sidelines doesn't make sense; I had no idea what sex was. I guess I was just a fan of it, like someone watching a foreign sport, completely unaware of the rules. Imagine watching cricket with a boner, and you get the idea.

The movies were borderline unwatchable dreck: sexual thrillers with thin plots and terrible acting. They showed real nudity, but the amount of endlessly terrible dialogue and contrived plot twists rarely made your time investment worth it. But the TV shows! The TV shows were the bread and butter: "Sin Cities," "Web Dreams," and the crown jewel of softcore porn: "Red Shoe Diaries." While the other shows were like well-made sedans, not the flashiest, but they'll get you where you need to go, Red Shoe always felt like a sexual Lamborghini: the ratio of erotica to plot was low, with as much time spent on character development as it was on a woman's bare ass. While full nudity was only ever implied, the constraints of a half-hour format guaranteed the first softcore sex scene usually happened in the first ten minutes, and who knows how many you'd get after that? Three? Five? This was peak titillation.

Is it possible for something to be hopelessly dated before you even shoot it? That had to be the intention with

Red Shoe Diaries. The look, the music, the genre, the round eyeglass frames; none of these trends had any hope of lasting, and yet still they managed to pump out five seasons and twenty movies in this inexplicable style. David Duchovny, who played the narrator, must have been blackmailed because that is the only reasonable explanation as to why he did this show for so long after he found success with The X-Files. Whenever it's brought up, he must cringe so hard he shits in his pants. I'm sure that one of the main reasons it was cancelled was due to the rising cost of renting lofts in Manhattan. More simply, perhaps the creators saw the breadth of their domain and wept, for there were no more softcore, pre-cum-stained worlds to conquer.

Eventually, Sigma's three month promotion came to an end, and we would bid it ado for another year. Scott White would hook up the coax cable into the back of the TV, and that was it for my Sigma sexual revolution. It was like going from the swinging '60s to the AIDS-fuelled paranoia of the mid-'80s with one trip to the local cable outlet. The glorious grey beast would come and go out of our household, and eventually, it would be replaced with a more generic cable box. The personality was sucked out: the sleek curves flattened, the keypad removed, and the size was reduced considerably. It went from being an event to just being a dinky box that sat on top of the TV. Truly the end of an era. Before the Sigma box, I was a boy, and after Friday Without Borders, I was a man.

OH NO, MY FAMILY HAS A 38 PERCENT ON ROTTEN TOMATOES!

The critics have spoken. I can no longer love my family.

I didn't need my family to be a critical darling to keep loving them, not by any stretch of the imagination, but a 38 percent review score on Rotten Tomatoes. That is abysmal. The review aggregate site's metacritic score puts us squarely in the Generally Unfavourable Reviews section with classics such as *"Hocus Pocus"* or *"Sister Act 2: Back In The Habit."* Oliver Fones of *The Observing* called us "middling," while Brian Ondorff of *Bluray.com* wrote that our family "aims to be cheeky and offbeat, but it's exhausting instead." How can I love these people as they are presently concocted in this family unit? My favourite flicks are critical darlings of the highest rapport. Flicks such as *12 Angry Men, The Maltese Falcon,* and *Paddington 2* (which I never actually saw, but I'll get to it and love it as the critics did) are classics. Untouchable. The sacred cows. But how did my family careen off into straight-to-video action movie territory?

First off, there are the individual performances. I don't want to gloss over anyone, but Dad didn't bring much to the table, literally or figuratively. His total lack of charisma since the death of his new wife was obvious to critics. Kenneth Kuran called him "by the numbers." I know there is a complicated man inside, filled with a raging hurricane made up of inner turmoil and grief, but none of that reads as he sits in the corner and politely makes conversation.

Mom is just ... bland. Loving, caring, strong, humble, empathetic, blah blah blah blah. “A mix of central casting stereotypes and an overly nostalgic scribe leaves little to contemplate in the end,” said Susan Abossa of the *Edmonton Sun*. You know what? I didn’t even notice it until I read that review. Crazy. Get an edge, Mom. You’re boring us to death.

Of course, that edge can cut both ways. At Thanksgiving last year, my brother Brilton, the police officer in training, jokingly began frisking my aunt after she inquired about his career path. We all laughed, but the frivolity didn’t last long as his search turned up an unmarked bottle of painkillers. Things got a bit rough as he produced handcuffs, and in response, my cousin began filming the event on his phone, much to Brilton’s ire. After restraining my 68-year-old aunt with a chokehold, he made some calls, and let's just say we won’t be seeing Aunt Phyllis for five to ten Thanksgivings. It could make for a good redemption arc if she handles it well, so there is some hope there. That usually plays on critics' heartstrings if it’s handled correctly. Abe Harrington of the *Junior Sentinel* tore the whole thing apart for being exploitative of the times we currently live in. I don’t disagree here; there is little nuance in rage, and Brilton is all rage. “Yes, you can yell, but should you?” Delise Holisten wrote in her scathing takedown of the scene on *dvd.org*.

What is the opposite of a stereotype? A nothing-type? That’s Grandpa for you. A big nothing. Too old for any real dramatic tension, he only exists and takes away from the family members around him, forcing us to endlessly repeat our benign pleasantries to him at increasingly louder volumes. Like ... hello? Maybe he should be trans or something. At the least, gift us with diversity while you drag down everyone else's individual performances to your incoherent level. No critic even took the time to dog his performance; I am doing it as a mission of mercy from the rest of the family.

As individuals, we are a letdown, but as an ensemble, we fall flat on our faces. I never thought we were *Gosford Park* (91% on the Tomatometer), but maybe we were a poor man's *Royal Tenenbaums* (81% on the Tomatometer*). But it turns out we are closer to a *Mars Attacks* (51%) or a *What To Expect When You're Expecting* (23%), which, to be fair, I thought was a stone-cold classic until the reviews told me otherwise.

The top-rated critical reactions to our family unit ranged from "awkward and cold" to "tense." Even eagle-eyed Rotten Tomatoes users could see it. "The long stretches where they all silently watched *Antique Hunters* on TV had little to no payoff," wrote user Romeo_Rodeo69. These are NOT the opinions of educated movie watchers; these are the people on the street with enough wherewithal to sit down and put thought and meaning into reviews that literally no one will ever take the time to read.

So what can we work on? For one thing, production values. Our house is dated and cheap-looking. I know we don't have a huge budget, but we (or specifically me, I suppose) have a large amount of time on our hands to invest in set design and prop selection. Perhaps we could add some thought to our wardrobe: Brilton is angry, so he wears a red shirt? This isn't high-level thinking, people, these are the basics, and if we follow through, maybe we can put some energy into our performances. Instead of watching *Antique Hunters,* maybe that useless sister of mine, Brittany, can bring home a POC, and we can get a conversation started. 65% ... no, 75% is in our grasp, people!

*81 percent? Are you fucking kidding me?

LOVELY QUAN

I had rehearsed the pronunciations again and again in my car right before I walked in. Watching the man in front of me bumble and butcher "Karaage," This fool. You could have practised. It's borderline racist I thought. I looked around as if I had said that out loud, and that people were agreeing with me. I, the great unifier, as they might one day refer to me, stepped up to the till to order my food. The woman's face smiled politely as I thoroughly mangled the Japanese language. How long will this painful memory haunt me? I wondered as I took a seat in the intimate waiting area of the ramen restaurant.

"15 minutes," the woman had said. 15 brutal minutes. Just me, this receipt, and my mind. My phone was in my car, the battery completely drained from me replaying a video to help me with my pronunciation of the Japanese word for chicken wings. So I busied myself with a familiar task: organizing my seemingly endless catalogue of worries. Lately, cardiac health had taken a back seat to Alzheimer's disease. This new, sexy bit of uneasiness had been brought on by the constant barrage of commercials detailing the disease and its various and frankly all too common symptoms. A sweet-looking older man begins buying four litres of milk seven days a week, or a woman in her 40's begins misplacing common items around the house. I do those kinds of things. I've done them today. I have a lot of coffee creamer in the fridge and I can never find my headphones. I was "self-diagnosed" and practically living with the disease at this point. In order to test how the condition had already ravaged my once young, able mind, I concocted a simple test: memorize the receipt, every piece of information, and recite it back to myself. The order number and restaurant name were easy. If I kept things simple, I could still function. This goddamn disease will not define me," I reasoned with myself. I'd moved down to the next line, "Server name," and below it "Quan."

To be honest, I hadn't noticed Quan while she was taking my order. I was too busy trying to maintain my composure after flubbing the Japanese word for deep-fried potato cakes. But now sitting in the cramped seat in that waiting area, I can't believe I didn't notice her. Her soft round face, seeming so plain a moment ago, was now radiant and beautiful. Her demeanour was unmistakably warm as she helped customers. Her smile was a bright splash of colour in the black and white confines of the minimalist Japanese restaurant.

As my wait continued, my interest in Quan became a quiet obsession. I studied her soft hands and flawless skin. I began to fall in love with the way her hair danced across her shoulders every time she turned to answer the phone or fill a customer's bag with napkins. I was on the edge of my seat every time she called out an order number, desperate to prolong our time together. Half hoping she would summon me to the till, and half hoping I would be allowed to wait here forever. Maybe when I get my order, I would complain, search for the smallest fault in my food and try to spark a conversation from there.

I imagined the first few months of our lives together. The butterflies in my stomach during our first few dates. Agreeable conversations and friendly energy every time one of us brings up a new topic. The way she would try to serve me and I would gentlemanly refuse, insisting that she “leave that business at work,” as I insist that she sit down and let me rub her sore feet. The sugary feeling of leaving her apartment knowing that I was special, at least to her.

As time moves on, things would become a little more serious. We have our first fight, it’s over something small and stupid, but at the same time, it’s big and important. A comment is taken out of context or an ill-timed facial expression is noticed and over-analyzed. The next time we speak, we’ll spend most of the time apologizing and laughing about how stupid it all was. We make fun of each other for overreacting and promise to talk things over next time. The promise is more important than either of us let on -- an unspoken understanding: This might be real.

After a while it becomes ordinary. Me and Quan. Quan and me. Our social circles will eventually become entwined and some will become unlikely friends or possibly lovers, while others fall by the wayside. We rearrange our lives around each other like living room furniture- some people are comforting like a well-worn chair, while others are discarded like a battered, water-ring covered coffee table.

I was jarred out of my fantasy by an errant elbow to my shoulder. The minuscule woman who delivered it apologized profusely. I had been too engulfed in my fantasy life with Quan that I hadn’t noticed the second leg of the dinner rush was in full swing. The waiting area was practically bursting at the seams and the air had become humid and thick. All of us sitting and waiting in our own little worlds, our minds escaping to other, happier places. I'd completely forgotten about my Alzheimer's diagnosis, which in itself is concerning. Carefully I studied the receipt again: Order number 23, Kintaro Ramen, Tebaski, server name, Quan, 1. Order number 23, Kintaro Ramen, Tebaski, server name, Quan, 1. Order number 23, Kintaro Ramen, Tebaski, server name, Quan, 1. Staring at the receipt, trying to lull myself back into my fantasy, I made a disturbing discovery: "Quan" was actually an abbreviation for "Quantity." The name that had so captivated me, the only thing I knew about this beautiful woman that I had built an entire life, an entire existence with, was a complete and total fabrication.

The speaker that was bolted onto the wall barked out my order number. Getting to my feet, I realized that I had a lump in my throat the size of a fist. I couldn't swallow. My palms were sweaty and my hands were trembling. My knees felt like they wouldn't buckle and I would crumble attempting my first step. Holding the brown take-out bag, she smiled the smile I had seen a hundred times in my fantasy, in our progeria life together, I'd experienced it for the last 15 minutes or so. Her expressive eyes glittered in the last bit of fading sunlight that crept through the window and I felt calm. She handed me my food and that's as close as my trembling hand would ever come to hers. Goodbye, my sweet Quan. Or, whatever your name is. Soon I would forget her entirely. Damn this disease.

THE NUDIST COLONY GETS AN ABOVE GROUND POOL

We rode in Cliff's beat-to-hell, pale green 1972 Chevy pickup truck. The other men laughed, but I was silent. To me, this was still offensively early in the morning, but to them, this was a regular Saturday. I was the youngest in the truck by three decades, yet these elder statesmen were beaming with energy that I could not muster at that hour. Cliff at the wheel, Scott the passenger, and Leslie sitting in the back with me were the regulars. The brains, the brawn, and the unorthodox problem solver. What did that make me? These road-worn skin dogs were already itching to get out of their cottons and denim, yet I was feeling nervous, bashful, and embarrassed even.

It wasn't my first rodeo with these vets; I've pulled some long hours on these highways the last few summers, but none had yet to lead me down this back road. As we pulled up to the massive walled compound, a burly man with a clipboard approached the driver's side window. He broke out into a smile when he recognized Cliff. They made a friendly exchange. It was an ordinary interaction, except that the man was completely naked. The tall wrought-iron gates, emblazoned with "It's 5 O'clock Somewhere," breathed a mechanical sigh and slowly began to open. That's when it got uncomfortable.

"Cliff's Lifts" had begun like any other above-ground pool business: a weekend venture made possible with the investment of wholesale above-ground pool kits and the infinite patience it takes to piece them together. But Cliff was different. He'd take any dirty job, and it bought him the reputation of a maverick. Any pool, any time, anywhere. It was the "where" that got him the good business.

As we pulled into the nudist colony, we were flagged into a processing area by a man and woman in hazmat suits. We were disrobed and deloused. Over the harsh sounds of the high-pressured water spraying against us, I could hear our toolboxes and personal items being rummaged through. Anything that resembled clothing was gathered and burned in a large pit. After processing was complete, we were escorted to the area that the nudists designated for their pool. Standing there nude, I felt jealous of the other men on the crew. They were so natural, so at peace with themselves. They were by no means Adonises, but they carried themselves with quiet confidence. They stood still, waiting to be instructed, occasionally spitting out sunflower seed shells. I'm not sure where they hid those when we came in, but I bet they didn't taste great.

We got to work. The early morning sun beat down hard, but the occasional breeze was nice. For the first hour or so, I managed to hide my dignity with the draping pockets of a tool belt. That was until a stern-faced man passing by in a golf cart whistled at me. He motioned with his hands to "spin it around," and I did, revealing my genitals to him. He nodded and drove away. This was a strange place indeed.

Aside from the occasional "pinch" when some wayward skin would get caught between a few pieces of metal, there was no downside to erecting the pool in the nude. It wasn't practical, but it was better than the Renaissance fair fiasco when they deemed that Scott's blood pressure medication wasn't authentic to the experience. It had made for a long day of work when they replaced all of our tools with rounded wooden mallets and period-appropriate hand-cranked drills.

Things were going fairly easy until a gust of wind at an inopportune time changed everything.

We were in the midst of a crucial section of pool construction, raising the walls of the pool that would act as the skin around its brittle skeleton. The wall was heavy, and it took everyone to get it into position. The age of my fellow constructors was beginning to become apparent as we mustered all of our might to push it up and into position. That's when the wind gust hit, and the whole operation went FUBAR. Raising my hands up, I caught the far section of the wall of the pool; Cliff and Scott caught the sections farther away, while Leslie was stuck on his back beside me, holding up his section of the wall with his legs. "I need a bolt to lock it in!" he called out to me, but I couldn't risk, even for the moment that it would take to lean down and toss him a bolt, in fear that we'd all be crushed by the wall I was already barely supporting.

"Use your dummy!" Leslie pleaded with me.

He was right. This was no time for shame. I began to move my hips in a circle, gaining momentum. I was dripping with sweat. Every muscle in my body was crinkled and on display now. I knew I only had the strength for one swing.

Scott concentrated hard on keeping the wall level, but Cliff cheered me on, knowing that I needed it and he didn't have the insurance to cover one of our injuries. I put every ounce of strength I had into my pelvis and swung my penis at the pile of bolts, sending them flying in every direction. By some miracle, Leslie had caught one out of the air and, quick as a cat, had the bolt installed, and the pressure on all of our arms lessened a bit.

Maybe it was having come close to being killed, or maybe it was the exhaustion, but for the rest of the afternoon I didn't feel nervous or ashamed of my body. I felt like myself. It felt great.

When the work was done for the day and we were loading up the truck , I took one last look at the colony. Silhouetted against the setting sun, still nude, Leslie leaned down and picked up a Coors Light can that was sitting on the side of the road. He crushed the two ends toward each other to fashion a pipe. He loaded a nugget of marijuana into the homemade chamber and lit it.

"Any dirty job," he said to himself, taking in a massive hit.

Where did he hide that weed? Where did it come from? Am I missing something?

MY SONS WISHED THAT DRAGONS WERE REAL AND NOW WE'RE ALL FUCKED

It's been a few months since this all started. My sons, my two beautiful boys, were up late being the curious, rambunctious kids that they are. Jumping about, fondling my fine antiques and whatnot. It had been a long day selling tridents over the phone and I needed some rest, and in a selfish effort to stifle their endless energy, I put into motion the events that would cost the world dearly. I used an old trick my Ba-Ba used on me when I was a recreant. I told them that if they made a wish at 11:11, it would come true, but only if they laid down in bed, shut their eyes and focused all of their energy on that wish.

Well, I'm sorry, everyone. They did just that and now we are totally, inarguably, fucked. It came on slowly, as these things usually do. Sketchy videos from China. Weird news reports from India. Images and words from sources I couldn't trust, and besides, it seemed like a distinctly "foreign" problem.

Well, just a week after "the wish," the dragons did indeed arrive stateside, and it got ugly quick. They were swooping down into busy streets and grabbing groups of pedestrians to fly off with them, destroying cars with their fiery breath and using our world like it was their toilet. I can't stress this enough: all they do is shit. Everyone acts like it isn't a big deal in the grand scheme of things, but it really is repulsive. I saw one of the gigantic male dragons drop a downright impressive amount of dung on the bus that I use for my commute. I wasn't on the bus at the time, lord knows I would have been crushed, but I saw it happen just two stops before mine. That was enough for me. I went straight home, where I found my two rambunctious boys giggling and laughing on the floor. Deep down I knew they had something to do with this.

I put it out of my mind and tried to move on with life in the most normal way that one can live their life with the skies full of goddamn terrifying mythical beasts everywhere. Walking into the office on the 58th floor one morning, I was met with a foul stench. They had been systematically taking over the tower I work in floor by floor for a few days and it seems they had finally reached ours. The office had become some kind of Dragon's Lair. Laying eggs, fucking, pooping (of course, all they seem to do is fucking poop) and generally hanging out doing dragon stuff. I grabbed my monthly leads under one arm and my coffee machine under the other and hightailed it out of there. It seemed I would be working from home until this situation cleared up.

"The economy," I thought as I hustled home. "What will this do to the economy!"

Well, I hate to brag, but for a while I was thriving. There had been some real capital gains to humanity's losses in this situation. Folks used to smirk at me when I would tell them what I did for a living, but nothing brings down one of these godless winged beasts like an American-made trident. I was hitting my quotas every week, with last quarter looking real bananas. The NFL was to start up again and they were planning to post a small army at every game to defend against any creature patrolling the skies. Every one of them would have an American-made trident in their hand; but alas, the first game was an unmitigated disaster. The dragons made quick work of those poor bastards and Monday nights will just never feel the same way again. As for me, I was laid off, but not before I added a few fortified towers and a moat to my home.

A small gig economy has also sprung up in this new world that has been thrust upon us. Need a man covered in deer piss to run the opposite way you're going in the vain hope that it will distract the dragons long enough for you to acquire your daily bread at the food depot? That'll cost you nine bucks. He's available all day.

Once it became clear that humanity had no answers for the dragon problem, I tried to fix what I did, to repair this world and hopefully return it to some order. I managed to wrangle my two beautiful, rambunctious boys before bedtime one night. By that point we were sleeping in shifts, of course, one of us always manning the arrow slit in tower two, but I pulled a double in an effort to salvage humankind. I sat them down and explained that they had to reverse their 11:11 wish, and get rid of the dragons. They counteroffered, and negotiations continued for some time. They are clever boys after all, both pre-law at Rutgers. But they relented, and when the time came, shut their eyes, made a wish, and focused all their energy on our species' future.

But, we're all still fucked. The boys have a high-end jet ski that they can't use and every day is Taco Tuesday, but the damn dragons are still out there, still killing people and running roughshod over humanity. We live our lives in fear. Fear of the skies. Fear of where the next gigantic poop will land.

It's the dragon's world now and we merely live in their toilet.

Stay safe.

CAMP HERO

In the peaceful town of Montauk, Long Island, stands a piece of history. A monument to one of man's greatest achievements, a commemoration of the full cooperation of science and military spending, and the extravagance of the human mind. Yet, at the same time, it is a simple radar dish.

Built to watch over the uncharted skies of the Midwest, surveying through the clouds for red freedom naysayers, the dish was decommissioned in 1954 due to the rising population in the area threatening its facade as a sleepy New England fishing town. The dish sat on its hill, an orphan reminder to middle America of the outlandish spending habits of the U.S. military.

Around 1961, enough "heat" from the Philadelphia Experiment had blown over to continue diving into more frivolous scientific research. With renowned outsider scientist Martin Kane at the helm, an unnamed project was presented to Congress. It was to be a facility that gathered the best scientific minds to explore the fields of time travel, meta-human experiments, subliminal message systems, aircraft prototypes, teleportation, bioengineering, and the melding of country music with rock 'n' roll. Having run out of space on the official form, Kane summed the research up as "General Scientific Boobery." The project was officially denied funding due to the astronomical expense but received discrete backing from an unnamed government think tank. Conspiracy theorists claim the funding could be traced to a cache of Nazi gold, worth roughly ten billion dollars, that was discovered by American troops in Northern Germany after the Second World War. Each member of the elite eight-man squadron that discovered the gold was meticulously assassinated utilizing clever and exciting methods. Those will not be discussed further here, but trust me when I say it was fucking gnarly.

The project was too large to house in the original three-bedroom apartment in which the Philadelphia Experiment was based and unfortunately, like in most fields, breakthroughs seldom occur without a giant radar dish to set the mood. The problem was rectified when it came to the attention of Congress that the fine people of Montauk had been telling the government to do something with the eyesore that the decaying radar dish had become or they would "burn it the fuck down." Under the guise of beautifying the decaying edifice to keep the locals happy, contractor Jerry Cole was brought in to design and build a subterranean facility in the hill underneath the radar dish to house Martin Kane's project.

What Cole brought to the project was as multi-layered as his performance on the solo album Bad by Myself that he would release months later. Some critics derided the album as a vanity project, but as time has passed, it has become something of a cult favourite for seedy government engineers. The housing of twelve subterranean floors dedicated to outsider scientific research was the first of its kind. The first ten levels housed their own departments, with two levels leftover for pet projects, empties, the occasional quinceañera, and some kick-ass chili cook-offs.

While some locals questioned why it took an army of men and equipment seven months of round-the-clock work to seemingly do nothing more than apply, poorly it's been added, a few coats of white paint to the radar dish, most were just happy that something had been done to the disgrace that had been lowering their property values for years. They slept peacefully, unaware of the radical scientific breakthroughs occurring in their own backyards. Martin Kane christened the facility "Camp Hero" after his favourite sandwich, and in 1961, the facility was opened.

When the government agreed to fund the project, Martin Kane claimed he would bring in the best scientists in their respective fields. This, along with many of the promises Kane had made, was a lie. He had an incurable penchant for hiring "bad boy scientists." Their out-of-the-box thinking and undeniable skill set came with rockstar attitudes. Fraudulent degrees, shady backgrounds, and an affinity for call girls were the norm among the group of hires that Kane made. Their actions would put a serious strain on the cover that was meticulously constructed by the government. People that owned the houses near the base would often complain about the cigarette butts thrown over their fences and the general vulgarity of the conversations overheard while scientists milled about out in the open on their breaks.

One of Martin Kane's more controversial ideas was the "Prank Wars" that began soon after Camp Hero opened.

The idea was to create some lighthearted fun and bonding between departments, and for a time was successful. The loud and jockish Meta-Human Division revelled in tormenting the outcasts comprising the Artificial Intelligence Department, once going as far as to send a drunken, partially invisible man (himself a victim of a failed experiment) to sabotage the AI scientists' cherished collection of pornography. The AI team held the upper hand, however, as self-aware defence turrets made short work of their partially visible foe. In retaliation, the invisible parts of the man were strewn throughout the offices of the Meta-Human floor, necessitating the use of high-level government janitors with cutting-edge thermal-goggle technology to sweep the area anytime the department was overwhelmingly malodorous with decaying flesh. Although the Meta-Human Division swore they'd get revenge, this incident was the official end of the "Prank Wars." The AI Division was declared the winner and, more importantly, got the babes.

Despite this semi-sanctioned buffoonery, legitimate breakthroughs were made at Camp Hero, specifically in the ESP department. Much of the town's homeless population volunteered for the projects. The promise of a cot, three squares a day, and all the cigarette butts they could scoop up proved too alluring for most. By bombarding the vagrant's "soul" with electromagnetic radiation, they found they could increase the subject's psychic abilities to such a point that many could simply produce objects out of thin air. Unfortunately, the objects produced were relatively "ho-hum" in the grand scheme of things. Automobile air filters and banana trees were the items most conjured from the beyond. To be fair to the volunteers, the scientists never thought to ask for anything else. The best thing the group was able to produce was high-quality speaker wire, much to the thrill of the audiophiles in the Jazz Division.

One subject, A-45, had failed after several attempts to produce a Mexican dinner for Camp Hero's Christmas party, instead only conjuring a pile of white dust. The scientist observing the experiment found the powder did not taste like Mexican food but noted that he was feeling "pretty rad" after snorting it. After a few weeks of productivity dropping and several of the scientists from the ESP Division flashing lots of cash, subject A-45 was terminated, and mandatory random drug tests were instituted in Camp Hero.

The extraterrestrial encounters department located in the eighth subfloor bore little growth in the period it was open. By 1966, the lab had several alien beings, but this was nothing new; in fact, aliens had been studied since the much-publicized Roswell incident. I won't bore readers with the details since they are so well known, but, briefly for the uninformed: A UFO full of Venus's best-looking aliens came to earth to compete in our bikini contests but ended up crashing their ship while trying to find an open liquor store in the dry county of Chaves, New Mexico. A passing Howard Hughes spotted the flaming wreckage and lured the aliens into his 1939 Electric Duesenberg with the promise of a good day's work for a good day's pay.

Like Hughes himself, the alien beings would spit on the floors and had little regard for the "house rules" that had been posted in the cafeteria. The only significant breakthrough Camp Hero made was the amassing of evidence that the alien culture was a rude and bitter one, which was thought to be to our advantage. They were so much like us, but assholes hate assholes and that's just the way she goes.

Between 1969 and 1973, the Time Travel Department was performing tests with something they called a "time tunnel." The science behind this great feat is shaded in mystery, due to the unique method employed by the department. What the group colloquially called "bangin' some shit around" was much like a jazz combo or the modern-day comedian. The scientists would get together and "jam" or "riff" on an idea. This technique has its place when you're hammering out a minor chord progression or explaining the difference between men and women to a crowd of yokels at the Laugh Hole in Andover, but it's considered irresponsible when working with antimatter and other dealings of the unknown.

What we do know from the various eyewitness accounts and filed reports is that the team accidentally harnessed a black hole. It was decided that Maurice, a lovable vagrant with an always positive attitude and a constant smile on his face, would be the first to travel through the time tunnel. His face lit up like he was helping the prison orphans on Christmas day when he heard the news. Confined to a wheelchair after having been hobbled the day before for trying to escape Camp Hero, Maurice was given a quick pep talk about what to expect, handed a tuna sandwich, and gingerly ghost-ridden into the perpetual black unknown. He never returned.

As months went by, the lazier scientists began throwing the contents of their wastebaskets into the hole, an activity that escalated to days spent tossing office supplies, children's toys, and empty liquor bottles, and, on the night of a rather spirited edition of the Camp Hero Christmas Party, a thunderous amount of human waste was evacuated into the void. What started out as a cheeky dare became routine by the following spring of 1972. During this time the chief scientist on the project, Dr. Felt, had been given the "Underground Scientist of the Year" award for the tunnel, a prize which in the early 70s consisted of twelve hundred dollars and a "sharp" red smoking jacket. While the money was appreciated (having assumed he was a shoo-in for the award months before, Dr. Felt had already put a $900 steak on a layaway plan and used the rest to get caught up on back alimony), the jacket was the true prize. He cherished it and went to great lengths to see that no harm came to it. It was the pride of the division, being the only piece of clothing without cigarette burns or bloody tissues stuffed into the pockets.

Months after Dr. Felt received his award, the time tunnel began to act up. The thousands of cigarette butts that had been carelessly tossed into the tunnel had started to come back out hundreds at a time. Crumpled paper, half-eaten sandwiches, and tossed pornographic magazines soon emerged from the void as well. One of the more distressing things found in the regurgitated trash was a piece of sandstone with what appeared to be a few lines of text. After careful analysis it was translated from ancient Sanskrit to read, “Seriously, are you fucking taking shits into this thing?” Unfortunately, this message was decoded too late, long after the annual Camp Hero Olympics and its marquee event, “Toss 200 Pounds of Warm Ground Beef into the Time Tunnel.”

It was in early April 1972 when amp Hero logged its first visit from the netherworld. Upon arriving at the office, the scientists gathered around the tunnel to fire their new company-issued pistols into the breast of the unknown. According to vague eyewitness reports, the tunnel began to wildly expand and contract before ultimately giving birth to a small purple creature that had been wounded by the aforementioned gunfire. Dr Felt reportedly removed his prized coat, wrapped the wounded creature in several towels, and bludgeoned it with his finest shovel. Witnesses claimed that just before leaving the facility with the creature stuffed in an old, weathered hockey bag, he proclaimed, “This isn’t the first hole I’ve dug in the desert, and Lord knows it won’t be the last.”

Later on in the day, after Dr. Felt had finished burying the first interdimensional being encountered by man, he returned to the office and found an alarming scene: spent shell casings, overturned furniture, the twisted disembowelled bodies of interns, and his favourite jazz records just like...strewn about without any respect. Realizing he’d breached protocol by leaving his gun at his desk, he reached for the nearest weapon, his finest shovel.

The following account is taken from the 1994 young adult novel "Felt You Coming: Dead Without Remorse" by Dr. Marvin Felt:

"Dr. Felt slipped through the hallways like a snake, the training was kicking in, there was no doubt about that. In times like these he was far more comfortable using his guile over brute force, but today's events had changed him. He looked forward to the blood, to the pain, to the battle, but a quick flash of Melissa's face entered his mind. That sunset, that moment they had at the boat launch. "There was no time to think of that now," he told himself. He peeked his head into the vault that contained the time tunnel and laid his eyes on the great purple beast. It towered nine feet tall and had a set of great ivory horns. It wore flowing liturgical robes and its hair was black and tangled like a cobra's nest. It made eye contact with Dr. Felt, there was no going back now. Bringing his mother's crucifix to his lips, he gave Jesus Christ a kiss and let his lord and savior fall back clumsily to his chest."

The novel sold poorly but received a boost in popularity when shock jock Howard Stern used pages from the book to wipe his ass with and then threw said pages at actress Elayne Boosler.

The true account was much less dramatic. In an effort to pump himself up for the ensuing battle, Dr. Felt repeatedly did key bumps of cocaine that later tested positive to be so pure it would "streak the most godawful hookers' hair white." The creature stood only 4'8 and was dressed more in a "bathrobe" than any ceremonial battle garb. Dr. Felt knew that the creature's one true weakness: Being bludgenied fifteen to twenty times in the head. He had the drop on the purple beast, who had busied itself trying to flip to side B of the The Weather Reports self titled album when Dr Felt, sweaty from numerous hits of cocaine, lost grip of the shovel when he raised it above his head. Falling to his knees, Dr. Felt begged for his life and offered many co-workers and even family members to stand in his place to be killed as a pittance. Reaching down, the creature ran his hands over Dr. Felt's beautiful, deep red smoking jacket.

"Sharp coat," it managed to say in garbled English. "Maybe...we make deal?"

What was learned in the following negotiations was that Maurice, the lovable vagrant-like character, had arrived in the creature's dimension and was immediately placed into observation. Maurice would regale his captors with tall tales of the vagrant lifestyle: living off the land, high-stakes bindle competitions, and goonie bat pummelling. He eventually rose to the rank of a leader due to his knowledge of the items that had been carelessly dumped into the time tunnel. With the various office supplies, he helped keep the dimension organized; with the human waste, he showed the beings how to plant crops; and with the hamburger, he showed them a "kick-ass" taco recipe. Maurice acted as an unofficial liaison for our dimension and often stressed that we were a loving and gentle species. Of course, this was before Dr. Felt had beaten the interstellar ambassador to death with his finest shovel. The being had meant no harm to humanity; it only wished to make contact with us to impart the secrets of his universe in exchange for knowledge of ours.

In an act of vengeance, the beast in the shabby bathrobe was sent through the time tunnel to destroy our hostile universe. Fortunately, for humanity's sake, the being had become quite smitten with Dr. Felt's smoking jacket, and a deal was brokered: the universe would be spared in exchange for Dr. Felt's smoking jacket and a conditional pair of slacks. The time tunnel would be, regrettably, disengaged, never to be opened again.

After the creature said his goodbyes and the time tunnel shuttered for the final time, Dr. Felt was overheard saying, "Only a universe of morons would worship a crippled hobo." A true asshole indeed.

Martin Kane itched for new breakthroughs but acquiring new programs presented a practical problem for Camp Hero: a shortage of space. Every floor had become occupied in the years since the facility opened, and there was simply nowhere for the facility to grow. One obvious option was to eliminate the floor housing the more established scientist's favourite candy bars, but this solution was defeated in a landslide when put to a vote. Martin Kane called a meeting with the most trusted members of his staff: a large teddy bear named Wallace and a full-length mirror. Save for a few cursory remarks, the bear was no help, and the full-length mirror only repeated what he said in a mocking fashion. Before boarding a plane to a private rehab facility, Martin Kane proclaimed that Camp Hero would purchase a trailer and park it behind a nearby grocery store.

So as not to arouse suspicion, a Camp Hero intern would tow the camouflaged trailer from the grocery store to a neighbouring park, where it would stay for the night. The scientists would be set free in the park until dawn. The new programs housed in the trailer, Quantum Physics and Cryonics, felt disrespected by their placement in the mobile home. And they were. A majority of their work was analyzing old reports, not exactly the "sexy" science Martin Kane thought he was getting in his drug-fuelled haze. The teams were seen as "fuddy-duddies" who would rather talk literature and politics than compete in the four-legged races and hot dog eating contests at the Camp Hero summer socials.

During a violent windstorm, the elaborate camouflage was torn off of the trailer. Weighing the cost of replacing the camouflage or selling the trailer outright for a profit, the newly sober Martin Kane shuttered both divisions, pocketed the $1,500 and immediately got drunk. The scientists and analysts were set free in the park one last time, and some say that on a quiet night, you can still hear them talking about boring things that no one cares about.

By 1975, Martin Kane's lifestyle started to put the future of Camp Hero in serious trouble. His dubious hiring practices continued when he spotted Arthur Collins while in line at a liquor store and insisted that he should check out his new car stereo. After agreeing that the stereo was loud, the men spent the next several hours drinking on the steps of the neighbourhood youth gymnasium while trading stories and yelling obscenities at teenage girls. The issue of employment had come up, and, by coincidence, Kane had been looking for a bright up-and-comer to head up the Robotics Division at Camp Hero. He offered Arthur the job on the spot. Arthur scoffed at the idea, as he possessed only a seventh-grade education and had recently turned sixty-seven years old. He eventually accepted the offer after losing a best-of-nine series of rock paper scissors.

What Arthur Collins would bring to the Robotics Division was invaluable: an astonishing lack of humanity. Scientists' wages were cut, as were holidays, sick days, and personal days. Arthur also forced them to cut all ties with the outside world and live in the Camp Hero facility. Once, an intern planned to sneak out to attend his mother's funeral. Arthur saw this as an act of betrayal and called in a bomb threat to the church where the funeral service was to be held, and the next night, Arthur blew up the church just to be safe. Months into this harsh schedule, which culminated in several scientists getting scurvy, the group decided to unionize. Upon hearing the decision, Arthur called his team into his office. He did not speak; instead, he silently punched a cement wall until he urinated in his pants. The word "union" was never uttered again.

Though one could argue with his methods, you could not argue with his success. What had been classified in the past as a group of second-rate toaster manufacturers was transformed by Arthur's iron fist into an unparalleled giant in the world of robotics. In seven short months, the division had gone from a mannequin hand with painted nails to a fully functioning autonomous android. An unmatched triumph in the field, capable of operating with pre-programmed behaviour, completely independent of human interaction. It was thought that the robot, over a long enough period of time, would learn dozens, if not hundreds, of skills, but the prototypes had unexpectedly limited shelf lives. The robotics team managed to embed basic human emotions into the prototypes, and as such, their short lives were filled with anxiety and fear, exacerbated by Arthur's drunken berating during routine examinations. After a thorough, top-down inspection, the robot would usually be reduced to a useless shell, either unable, or more likely, unwilling to continue operating in such a cruel, twisted environment.

There were many theories regarding the root of Arthur's monstrosity. Some say he was hard on the scientist and prototypes because his son Dylan had lost his legs in a motorcycle accident and Arthur wished to see him walk again so Dylan could move out. Little is known about his life before Camp Hero, and even less is known about it after he left. One morning he was just gone. Arthur Collins would be the last of his kind at Camp Hero. Changes were coming–in part because Camp Hero was out of money.

As it turns out, Martin Kane had been fuelling twenty-plus years of his rock 'n' roll lifestyle by skimming off of the Camp Hero budget. It should have been made apparent to the authorities when Kane tried to pay for a bottle of Mad Dog 20/20 with a gold bar emblazoned with a swastika. Between Kane's skimming, the unchecked budgets, and out-of-control spending, the Nazi gold cache was depleted. In February 1980, Martin Kane bleached his hair, bought a plane ticket for Venezuela, and was never heard from again.

The remaining funding from the government was a pittance compared to the seemingly unlimited budget Camp Hero had operated with for the first twenty years of its existence. Congress had changed significantly over the years. Sympathy, understanding, and negotiation ruled the day. Nanotechnology that could eat a human being from the inside out and reduce them to a pile of sausage casings was no longer desired, although the testing had been extremely successful. It was a new era of "mean people suck," and the research team at Camp Hero was full of inarguably mean people.

The robotics lab and the Time Travel Department had especially bitchin' parties before closing and tossed most of their equipment and classified documents into the unlocked Loomis bin behind a nearby apartment building. The office space was rented out, and the first six floors were soon occupied with catalogue sales and service. Science was no longer the priority–sales, sales, sales was now Camp Hero's edict.

The bottom six floors were all that remained dedicated to science. While evicting the shuttered Archaeology Division, it was discovered that they had been digging into the foundation of the Camp Hero complex. Whenever the team hit a water or, more commonly, a sewer line, the team would usually "pack it in for the day." The bottom four floors were declared condemned. The departments that were deemed cost-effective occupied the remaining two floors that were still available. The cloning department saved money by replicating the same scientist over and over to build a sizable staff while only paying out a single paycheque. This was heralded as a major “breakthrough in the workforce.” The program was shut down after being heralded by others as “White Slavery.”

But as the past slipped into the present, the era of over-the-phone customer service gave way to the internet, which, coincidentally, had been conceived at Camp Hero as a library system for the freakier scientist’s extreme pornography; the call centres and catalogue services ran out their leases and packed up. The foundation of Camp Hero had decayed to such a degree that it was cheaper to fill in the levels with concrete than to fix. Any scientific subjects still living at the complex were released to the public, leading to many humorous internet videos. Camp Hero was closed.

Now renowned as a kick-ass party spot, all that remains of Camp Hero is the radar dish. Teenagers can often be found congregating at “The Dish” on warm summer nights. Drinking, smoking pot and finger-fucking each other, they are oblivious to the scientific breakthroughs made by Martin Kane and his band of scientific miscreants that occurred in the subterranean complex beneath their feet.

I WAS A FUCK BOY AND NOW I'M A FUCK MAN

Friends, I stand at a fork in my, so far experienced anyway, marvellous road. To the right takes me down the same ol' dusty trail that I've been on. Protein shakes. Trend chasing. Days spent in strange beds with only brief respites to the gym. The other road, the strange one that brings me so much anxiety, could lead to so much more, but also toward my own ruin. Is it better to dance in today's fire or contemplate tomorrow's ashes? I take a few steps in one direction and lose my confidence. I stumble and teeter, tip-toeing from one path to another. Do I continue as a Fuck Boy, or do I ascend to a Fuck Man?

You may be familiar with a fuck boy. We haunt the malls and the nicer avenues. If there is a neighbourhood with a manicured median separating the two sides of the street, chances are you will find boys of my ilk patrolling like old-timey beat cops, smacking our batons in the palms of our hands and using location services on our phones to slip into nearby woman's DM's. We are smooth. We are sly. We don't have any money for rent, and we will gladly live with you and your parents and eat all the food in the house in our insatiable quest for protein. Chances are we swim or do some other totally useless activity that allows us to wear as close to nothing as possible. We make average men's eyes roll because they want to be us and encourage the indifference of the women who simply cannot be with us.

I come from a long line of fuck boys. My great- great- great- great- great- great- great- granddad was a fuck boy of much renown in the old country. Legend has it that he convinced, passive-aggressively of course, that one of the women he was courting should dye his then- beige peasant rags with blueberries. Then, and using the supposed clout of colour, he talked his way onto the Mayflower and became the first fuck boy in America.

Another great-great so-and-so in my lineage was a fuck boy of Eva Braun before she met the ultimate fuck boy (we don't talk about that guy tho). A cousin fuckboy of mine was supposed to be the 20th hijacker on 9/11, but he slept in after making his way into a party hosted by Steven Soderberg the night before and simply couldn't be bothered to wake up on time and handle his supposed "tasks" (much respect). I don't mean to brag; I'm just saying my fuck boy roots run deep.

But why change? Why give this all up? All of the fuck boys I mentioned in my family died the same way: penniless, alone and shooting dust (much respect for that though). Cut down at their knees in their prime and reduced to being Work Boys or Errand Boys. Aside from fighting tradition, I see the face that is staring back at me in the mirror: An aging one, starting to wrinkle and grey. When the MILFs become your peers, it's time to reevaluate. It's time to ascend to the next level: The Fuck Man. This involves commemoration.

I must find four fuck men to vouch for me. We spend a day at an exclusive (expensive though) Fuck Man Spa where we ritual. First, I will sit and listen to their fuck man accounts of the past. They are a storytelling people, after all, because they cannot be bothered to write anything down. Next, our bodies alternate from extreme hot to extreme cold. We are battered with plantain leaves for hours, and our faces are rubbed with gourds. Our towels are small, and we all look really great in them (just thought I'd throw that in there), and I spend the evening dancing in the vapours of their experience, inhaling what I can. Mind. Body. Spirit. Fuck Man Awesomeness. Early the next morning, they take their helicopter to view the sunrise and make their decision.

If I'm accepted, there is a lot of responsibility. I'm not sponging off Instagram influencers and getting dirty looks from their parents when I put the finished apple juice container back in the fridge anymore. I will receive a swanky condo or possibly a loft space and the mortgage that comes with it. I will be assigned a high-paying job in advertising or promotions. The kind of position that is ninety percent gesticulation, eight percent smiling and two percent "vibes.".

I'd also need a fuck man name like Jacob or Simon. I need to burn all of my fuck boy clothes and replace them with fuck man suits and $400 casual t-shirts. To do that, I will need to go to a fuck man bank and speak to a fuck man banker and get a fuck man line of credit.

If approved, I will be engulfed by the inner sanctum. I might not rub elbows with fuck men hall of famers like Hugh Grant, Leo Dicap, and Billy Zane, but I am guaranteed some face time with modern masters such as Zac Efron, John Mayer or Dennis Long Legs (Dennis isn't famous, he just is really tall and has a friggin' bitchin' nickname). In a few years, maybe I could mentor a young fuck boy and have him inhale my vapours as I have inhaled before me. I will grab him by the hand and lead him down the same fork in the road I'm about to walk down. Another generation of Fuck Men, being sexy but, above all, being mostly useless.

POST-HALLOWEEN REPORT: MY GABBA GHOUL COSTUME WAS A FLOP

Well, it pains me to say this, but you were all right. Yes, I heard all of your concerns but I continued on undeterred. Three Halloween parties. Three. And despite all my efforts, my brilliant costume was an unprecedented flop. The legend of the Gabba Ghoul will go down in history as one of the worst Halloween blunders in my career.

The night began with so much hope. Staring at myself in the mirror with $275 worth of cured meat stapled to a white robe, I carefully adjusted the "Scream" mask that I artfully airbrushed in the style of an Italian cold cut. Damn. I was looking good. Surely the general public would gush over the cleverness of my costume. It was the right time, that's for sure. The Sopranos was back in the pop culture lexicon and after a year of cancelled Halloween parties, people were gathering in person and ready to check out each other's pop-culture-influenced costumes. "This is gonna be huge," I whispered to myself, flattening the various cold cuts dangling from my body. Hours later I found myself speeding to the next party, completely shaken to my core. I had become overtaken by the smell of meat and was forced to unroll every window in my car. I assumed it was the salt and nitrates from the cold cuts that had me feeling faint, but looking back now, it's clear it wasn't the smell of salami, it was the stench of failure.

In my defence, I felt I could do no wrong after the Halloween Zoom party the year before. My costume, "Tony the Tiger King," had been an unadulterated hit. Screenshots of my elaborate orange and black body paint, sunglasses, and mullet had been all over Instagram for almost a week. The likes and mentions came rolling in and I have to say: it felt good. It felt like the culmination of years upon years of grinding out pop culture Halloween costumes that were wasted on poorly attended house parties or lame work functions. All the toiling had been worth it. The internet opened its large arms and let me into their warm inner sanctum.

So what happened this year? I think it was the pressure. Coming down from Tony the Tiger King took months. I decided to ride the success of the costume and just enjoy the moment before concocting the next great viral Halloween outfit. After all, next year's spooky celebration seemed so far away. But the months passed quickly and I felt like I was in a creative dry spell. Before I knew it the colours on the trees were changing and it was September. I was sweating bullets. I racked my brain for weeks, the stress got so bad I made the difficult decision to take a leave from my work at the chicken plant. And if anyone knows me, they know that my other passion in life is my work at the chicken plant.

I knew I wanted to go meat-based. It was a gut feeling. My first instinct was David

Bo-Loney, my sandwich meat take on David Bowie, but I found the product too slippery to handle and ultimately too unpredictable to apply to my face in the fashion that Mr. Bowie had on the cover of “Aladdin Sane.” The drawing board was pretty empty when I opened up Twitter for some inspiration. I came across an account that subtitled socialist ideas over Soprano’s screen grabs. I was trying to understand why millions of people followed this account when it hit me. I leapt in the air, knocking all the baloney to the ground, but I didn’t care. My meats would be salted, not wet and unpliable. I would be the “Gabba Ghoul.” I RSVP’d to every Halloween party I could find.

The second party was worse than the first. Maybe the Gabba Ghoul was too high-concept. Maybe it’s because the homeowner yelled at me when I stained the couch and the chair in the living room when I sat down to relax. These people were basically strangers after all, and I had barged into their home with my cured meat dangling everywhere. Every conversation was the same: me explaining what the costume was, even at one point resorting to writing it out on a piece of paper to show how clever it was. I think I got a few people to check out The Sopranos, but no one laughed, guffawed or wanted a picture of me. I was in one group photo on Instagram, but the lighting was so bad that I looked like Edgar Winter in a fur coat.

Despite everyone's scorn, I still felt that my creativity should be acknowledged. All the low-rent costumes in the house and I was the one made to feel bad? Yeah, cute pirate outfit, Bonnie. Oh! The Joker? Did you get tired of dressing like The Crow, you loser? But in the end, these raging emotions left me nowhere but sucking air through my open car window and feeling bad for myself.

The third party. The one with the dog. I don't even want to talk about that. That animal won't be shitting solid for a week and I'm confined to this goddamn bed till the streptococcus clears up, which is kind of a coincidence because I thought that was an Italian cold cut for the longest time.

So, folks, I'm taking next Halloween off. This is not defeat, though. This is a recharge. I put everything I had into the Gabba Ghoul. My time, my stress, and my passions all went into this costume. But next Halloween, do me a favour: Find the person who isn't satisfied buying a costume off of a shelf, even if they missed the mark a bit, and tell them, "Good job," or "I totally get that weird thing you're talking about." It'll make a world of difference. This is the Gabba Ghoul signing off.

MICROWAVE TIME

It's the first thing in the morning. You get into your car. No worries, you have plenty of time. You fire up the engine and look at the dashboard. Panic. You could have sworn you had a few more minutes. At least 5. What's going on?

You're running on microwave time. My time.

I am a clock on cocaine. You can't trust me. You can reset my time as often as you'd like, but I'll never keep it. I run fast. Because I am the appliance of the fucking future. I want your day to be over sooner so you can come back home and admire the piece of military-grade cooking precision that is me.

Maybe you should look at the stove once in a while if you want to plan out your day. It keeps pretty good time. I mean, it's no Big Ben, but it'll do. But you don't want to. The stove is a boring asshole. It's like having your nagging parent as an appliance. Always beeping about this and that, telling you when it's ready for you to put the food in. You can just pop me open and slide in that food whenever; I'm always ready to go. And let's be honest, between you and me, the stove peaked in the 50s, and it's too stupid to figure it out. Nice heating elements, Grandpa. You ever hear of evolving?

Me? I just run on this little thing called RADIATION. Maybe you've heard of it? It pretty much ended World War II by terrifying that scumbag Hitler so bad that he shit his unterhosen before planting a bullet in his brain. It helps turn cancer cells on themselves and saves millions of lives every year. But my awesome power scares people sometimes. Yeah, sales were bad after Chernobyl, but that was a huge misunderstanding. Don't throw the baby out with the bathwater.

"I don't even OWN one of those things," you'll hear people scoff, desperately trying to sound interesting to their equally insufferable friends. I have it on good authority that, secretly, those people do in fact microwave, and they microwave hard and way more than anyone should. I'm not here to name names, so it's best that I leave it at that.

There are other complaints that are valid.

"It cooks a little unevenly."

Yeah, well, like, maybe you should stir your fucking food once in a while?

"It doesn't defrost meat well."

You got me there. But in my defence, when you're a hammer, everything looks like a nail, and when you're basically a goddamn nuclear device, it's hard to "kind of cook, but not really cook the meat." I'll own up to that. I don't have time for your half measures; leave that up that idiot stove. Did you know that the stove's favourite TV show is The Big Bang Theory? I swear to the appliance gods that it is like living with your grandfather. The fridge is cool, though. It irks me sometimes, but we have a good working relationship.

Maybe you could learn a thing or two from microwave time. People are always rushing around, and for what? On your best days, you end up at home with me. Warm and cozy, watching some prestige TV with a nice steaming pile of freshly microwaved food that might be cold in the middle because you are too stupid, or lazy, to stir it halfway through the cook time. It's all we really want.

So, the next time you show up late and someone gets angry or even has the gall to tap their watch, tell them, "I'm on microwave time."

JOKE'S ON YOU, APRIL FOOLS DAY MAKES ME CRAZY HORNY

Tomorrow is going to be a rough day. Sure, I'll have my breathing techniques and some safe spaces I can get to in a pinch, but other than that, it's just me and the prank crew at work. Those hot-ass tricksters. It's been a few years since I've had to face this. During the "uncertain times" I was safe at home. Spared from the cling film-covered toilet seats and the whoopie cushions in the break room, I lived without fear in my controlled environment. But, a few weeks ago when the email came in confirming our return to the workplace, my first thoughts were of April Fool's Day.

I'm not sure why, but the day, and the antics that come with it, make me crazy horny.

In the past, I sought a remedy, some kind of antidote to this damn concupiscent day. Exposure therapy wasn't all it was cracked up to be and the therapist I was seeing ended up having to tear the carpets in his office out. Companies claimed they could get rid of the stains, but they would never be truly clean. Next was the holistic approach. The last I heard, poor Danica was locked in an insane asylum, endlessly carving "April Fool" into the walls with her fingers until the nails wore down to a bloodied stump.

I decided that distance was the only cure. At the age of 21, I boarded any number of planes and trains to get away from society. I could run, but I could never get far enough away. I had been illegally harvesting ketchu in the darkest heart of the Congo when I felt the unmistakable burning on my ankle that could only be a symptom of what the locals colloquially refer to as "pied chaud" or "hot foot." Dancing around in the fields, attempting to extinguish the flames at my feet, I bit my lip hard to control the moans that were trying to erupt from inside of me while the locals chortled and slapped each other on the back. On the remote island of Tristan da Cunha, I had lost track of the days until I opened an envelope full of glitter and instantly became fully engorged. The Nebraska Sand Hills, the Ténéré Desert, and the ice fields of Oymyakon, Russia. These places where I managed to find my peace were all eventually sullied by the stink bombs, fake vomit, and itching powder that turned my sexual crank in a downright dangerous way.

I knew that when Israel adopted the day, it was time to leave, to grab my backpack and emerge from the dust back to Western civilization, and return home to a land of sexy handshake buzzers and Vaseline-covered door handles. There was simply nowhere else to go. Possibly Antarctica? But even the sternest science crews will have a joker that is keen to leave a faux poop on a countertop somewhere. The world will not let me leave this libidinous day behind.

Maybe that's not the right attitude. Maybe it's time to stop running, to stop trying to fix myself. I'll run into the morning meeting and yell, "This day is extremely erotic for me, so I'll be using the nap room frequently. Deal with it." I can no longer live in shame. Bring on your caramelized onions, your post-it note bombs, your fake excrement, and whatever else you got. I'm here, I'm horny, and the joke's on you.

WHITE PEOPLE WITH DREADLOCKS ANONYMOUS

The room was full tonight. Old. Young. A businessman. A slacker. A soccer mom. Our pale faces looked exceptionally grim under the unforgiving fluorescent lights. Roger, a heavyset man in his 40s, was getting to the climax of an all too familiar tale.

"I don't know who needs to hear this today, but it's never too late. Never too late to put that bong down, take off that tie-dye T-shirt and...and do what you have to do." Roger did a silent "Thank you" and collapsed back into his chair.

The dimly lit multi-purpose room was the ultimate stereotype of AA meeting rooms. The grease-stained box of donuts. The awful coffee that always tastes burnt, no matter how fresh it was. It was all laid out on a gray folding table that, if it could speak, would be begging to be put out of its misery before it was forced to hear another heartbreaking tale. The posterior destroying metal folding chairs, the kind that was now craning under Roger's considerable weight, were prepared in an imperfect circle, arranged so that the participants felt compelled to share their stories. I ran my hand over my freshly shaved head. It was my first meeting.

The night continued in this fashion for the next hour or so. Every person reciting a different version of the same story.

“We have a new person in the group tonight,” Reese, the group leader, said before the meeting was coming to an end. “I was wondering if he wanted to introduce himself and maybe say a few words.” I wasn’t planning on speaking tonight, but Reese’s generous, welcoming smile raised me to my feet.

“I’m Rowan”

“Hi Rowan,” the group responded without enthusiasm. I took a deep breath. Time to cleanse.

“And I was a white person with dreadlocks.”

Everyone in the room nodded. They nodded that nod.

“I’m not going to bore you with my story because it is a lot like the ones you’ve already heard tonight. We were born, we grew up, and for some, like Ruby, it was a Phish concert.” Ruby, a woman in her late 30s, smiled and nodded rhythmically. She was digging this monologue like a golden era Mike Gordon bass line. I continued, “Or it was a Bob Marley greatest hits album, like Roy, or it was staring at the reflection of myself in the mirror wearing a brand new puka shell necklace. Our stories all started so innocently and ended in the same shameful way.” Roger’s face contorted into a red ugly mass of tears and pain. I crossed the circle and placed a hand on his shoulder as the man wept.

"I was so gross. And I looked so goddamn dumb!" he cried.

"We were all gross," I said gently.

"And we were all goddamned dumb! But not anymore!" I yelled. The once docile group had been pulled to the edge of their seats. "Three days ago, I looked in the mirror, looked at myself, at the people I have let down in my life, and I freed myself from bad choices." I paused for a moment and rubbed my freshly shaven head. "And I REFUSE to accept the idea that because I had dreadlocks once, I will have dreadlocks forever!" And with that statement, as if on cue, the room exhaled a collective sigh and slumped back into their seats. I looked around, confused. Reese, the leader of the meeting, stood up.

"Rowan, we've all been where you are. The first few days of an exciting change in your life." He looked around the room.

"Ruby, how did you feel the day after you cut your dreadlocks off?"

"Different. Powerful. Free."

"And how did you feel two weeks later?"

Ruby paused for a second and thought. "Lost," she said solemnly.

"Exactly, having dreadlocks when you are white is not a hairstyle. It's an illness. One that can never be cured, but can be arrested." Reaching into his pocket, Reese produced a small rock.

"Is that your..." I searched for the correct term. "...higher power?"

Confused, Reese replied, "No...no of course not. This is a crystal. A healing crystal."

I let out a snort of laughter that I quickly stifled.

"I'm sorry it's just—"

"No, it's fine. The crystals are my dreadlocks now."

"But that's just kind of...stup—"

"Yes, stupid. Of course it's stupid. But it's a stupid thing that I can keep in my pocket instead of on top of my head. Ruby, what's the stupid thing you do instead of having dreadlocks?"

"Oh, come on, you know." Ruby half-giggled.

"Come on, Rubes," Reese replied in a mock serious tone.

"Tarot cards."

"Annnnd?"

"A little bit of witchcraft."

Everyone in the room laughed. Reese moved to another person in the circle. "What about you, Randy?"

"I listen to The Red Hot Chili Peppers." The audience collectively "oofed." "Only on headphones," Randy added, trying to salvage some of his dignity.

"Astrology, even the moon signs and birth charts!" one voice added. "I make jewellery and sell it anonymously on the internet!" Spoke up another tortured soul, and with that, the group began talking amongst themselves. About the stupid things they do.

Focusing his attention back to me, Reese continued his point, “Maybe we replaced a vice for a vice, but at least it’s an embarrassing vice that people don’t have to see all the time.”

I grasped for the words, the fragment of the idea forming in my head.

“You can cut off the dreadlocks on the outside...”

“Yesssss...” Reese said, feeling a revelation coming on.

“But you can never cut off the deadlocks on the inside.” Reese slapped me gently on the shoulder.

“Welcome to recovery, my friend.”

MEDITATING ON THE WIND WITH THOMAS UGLYWEINER

There is a stretch of the PCH between the hippy-dippy scene of Sanny Frisco and the "look at me" spectacle of LA-LA Land that I always look forward to. The winding road bends her leg straight, and you're free to put your foot down and feel the purr of the engine. Today, the top is down on my 1971 Mercedes-Benz SL. September's early afternoon sun is shining. My leather driving gloves tickle the steering wheel in time with "Aqualung" that blares out of the stereo. It is a good day to be Thomas UglyWeiner.

"Mr. UglyWeiner! Mr. UglyWeiner!" my secretary called after me as I tried to sneak out of the office this morning. "Mr. UglyWeiner is my father's name," I said with a wink. She will be thoroughly reprimanded, of course. Sure, I'm pretty hard on my subordinates, but that's nothing when compared to a business negosh.

"Don't fuck with that UglyWeiner," they all say after eighteen rounds with this shark. Shark killer? Lost in my metaphors again. The true curse of the UglyWeiners: our grand imaginations.

There's a bit of construction coming up, but nothing can bum out this vibe. The high from a few sneaky tokes is lingering. Cherry blaster, high crust values, and I'm very toasted. This UglyWeiner is melting like a piece of cheese on a Philadelphia smash burger. I'm dripping on the grill, and Daddy don't know why. "Excuse me while I kiss this guy," I whisper to myself, quoting the incredible James Marshall Hendrix. Instinctively, my hand falls out the window and immediately finds the perfect harmony between fighting the wind and being one with it. It worms its way through the air as smooth as the rubber on the PCH.

It's not always September sun and classic rock for Thomas UglyWeiner. There have been dark days, too. The merciless bullies in my private school always find new things to rhyme with my unfortunate name. "Bombas Thomas!" They would yell as I walked down the hallways. They were clever. They were cruel. But now they shake with fear when the name UglyWeiner fills their ears and unloads on their demented faces. Or me and my brother, Amos UglyWeiner, scared to death of the dark after Mother UglyWeiner tucked us in tight at bedtime. Just a couple of UglyWeiners hiding under the blanket, shaking until the sun came up. "Good morning, UglyWeiners!" our housekeeper, Debbie Maggots would holler as we crept out of our protective shield, safe in the morning sun. A new day begging for two UglyWeiners to come out and play. A sun not unlike today's.

I'm climbing now. My car moves up the bends of the mighty PCH like a mountain lion. On each side of the highway, the drop is substantial, but like an apex predator, my classic vehicle ascends higher and higher with great ease. An UglyWeiner mobile is ready to explode into the sky and leave streaks across the great skyline of San Jose, leaving it scarred. Leaving it perfect.

As I pull into the parking lot of "UglyWeiner's Ojija Board Emporium," past the statues of all the great UglyWeiners that came before me, my mind is clear. My meditation left with the wind.

DEAD MAN WALKIN'

Fourteen years ago, I put ketchup on a hotdog, and now I'm on death row in a supermax prison.

Chicago. The mid-aughts. I found myself wandering through streets while traveling on business. My wife Mary would always say, "People don't want to buy brooms from a door-to-door salesman in 2008," but I disagree. Holding out your pen, looking a man in the eye, and waiting for him to sign on the dotted line is a high that I have never been able to match. And likewise, in eight to twelve weeks, when that man receives their broom, he will be reborn in the flex of our patented bristles. When he gathers that first bit of refuse, when he feels that stiff flex, no matter where I am, I feel a chill, and we are connected in that moment. Door-to-door broom salesman. There is fucking nothing like it.

I digress. I do that sometimes now, sitting here in my 4x8 cell, staring into the darkness, looking around at all the possible piles of dirt that could be swept. Back on that regrettable day, I had worked up quite the appetite, moving in and out of the revolving doors peddling my wares. Michigan Avenue was wet and cold, and between the rain hitting the ground and the sea of people around me, I felt overwhelmed. Not used to the big city hustle and bustle, I ducked into Traditional Ray's Traditional Hotdogs. I could have chosen anywhere, any hole in the wall to fill my gullet, but being a mark for family values of yesteryear, Ray's doorway was ordinary but extraordinary to me all at once. I stepped through one universe and into another. I hope there is another me out there who looked at Ray's tattered sign and dingy windows and went to anywhere else on that long, cold, wet street.

"Could I get some ketchup?" I asked, perplexed. The condiment bar had everything a hungry man could ask for, but no ketchup. "Ket...chup," I repeated, staggering the syllables to the confused woman behind the counter. She rolled her eyes and turned to the next person in line.

I looked at my bare wiener. What are my options? Mustard. Relish. Yuck! Too ethnic for my humble tastes. No one needs that kind of unnecessary shock to the system when they are trying to bite into a piece of great American folklore. I contemplated tossing the dog into the garbage, but I just couldn't. What would my dad say if I threw a perfectly good hotdog away? Probably something racist, but there certainly would be a lesson if you stripped away all those words you can't say anymore. I felt lost. My useless hotdog. My useless life. It was like staring into a funhouse mirror. What happened to me? I've pissed it away on selling brooms and . . .

But then I remembered my traveller! I patted myself up and down, hoping I had the presence of mind to bring it with me when, yes! Front left pocket. Right beside my heart. I pulled it out, and the room gasped. The novelty-sized ketchup bottle hung off my Swiss Army knife. Can't take it on a plane? Well, fuck you, TSA, and fuck you, Dad, because I'm in the driver's seat of my life, and if I want to sell brooms door to door and take a tiny bottle of ketchup with me on the airplane, then I will!

My bravado was out of control. With great flair I covered my soggy wiener with that delicious sugary goop. Lost in my own world, I didn't notice what was happening around me, and what that was was an alarming amount of nothing. The hustle. The bustle. It had all stopped. Rudimentary phones with rudimentary cameras snapped pictures of a rudimentary man trying to enjoy a hot dog any damn way he pleased. I tossed the empty traveller of ketchup into the garbage, pulled my raincoat hood over my head and walked out of Ray's hot dogs.

The rain kept coming down all afternoon, but I managed to press some flesh with a few potential sweepers. As I came to the intersection of State and Madison, I noticed a healthy police presence. My eyes shifted from a few frantic-looking beat cops to a regal-looking police officer on a horse. They were holding papers, trying to keep them from tearing in the rain. Their eyes went from the paper to each passing person. I felt a lump in my throat. Something wasn't right. They were on the hunt for someone.

I ducked my head down and passed the officer on horseback, but that only drew more attention. The rain was hitting my hood so hard I didn't hear him shout at me, but I knew. As I passed him, I turned my head and got a look at the piece of paper they had been studying. It was a sketch of a man, the same man I see in the mirror every day.

I was lucky. The rain. The traffic. The confusion. I managed to slip away, using alleys and dumb luck. At one point, I felt the heat coming around the corner, and I ducked into a small liquor store. I got myself a bottle of 101-proof Wild Turkey. Having paid, the kind man behind the counter allowed me to take my time and watch through the window. Maybe he thought I was waiting out the weather. Maybe he thought I had nothing else to do but watch the rain. Maybe he knew I was on the run, and this bottle of Wild Turkey was the only safe place I had left to crawl into. As the sirens and lights passed by, I nodded my head to him and left. The next thing I knew I was on the ground, my face pressed hard into the concrete. Men yelling. Calling me an animal, shaking an evidence bag in my face.

The rest of the legal process was a blur; some called it a kangaroo court. Some called it justice. I called it Tuesday or Wednesday or whatever day it happened to be. And now here I am, sitting in a cramped cell, pooping into a shiny toilet, trying to get updates about the new and exciting brooms out in that big scary world.

Like many of the needy, I was rude. Like some of the needy, I took. And like all of the needy, I needed. But it was just ketchup on a hot dog. What the fuck is wrong with people?

SEX ED

Neil sits in his child's cluttered bedroom. The floor is littered with soft plush toys and books. It's an ordinary children's room; the walls are a pale orange colour, and the top of the dresser is filled with snow globes and music boxes. In the middle of the room is a large, beaten-up wooden easel. With its rough edges and pad of weathered-yellow paper, it sticks out from the newer, pastel-coloured furniture.

The small bed Neil sits on is barely big enough for his five-year-old daughter, let alone a full-grown man, and it creaks under him whenever he shifts his weight. Uncomfortable, and fearing the bed might collapse, he stands just as his daughter, Veronica, enters the room. Neil motions for the young girl to take a seat on the bed, and once it's apparent he has her full attention, he begins his presentation.

"Your mother and I talked it over," Neil begins, obviously nervous, "and after seeing the . . . conditions of the public school system, we've decided to teach you about the birds and bees ourselves. So..." Neil winces as he flips the first giant sheet of paper on the easel and exposes a medical drawing of both the female and male reproductive organs.

The different shades of brown in the drawings are indicative of the 1970s.

"One day, in a long time, you'll meet someone you love, and you'll want to express that love by having sex." Neil is gaining some confidence now, but of course, none of this registers on the child's face. She is too young to even understand the basic principles of sex.

"Sex can be a beautiful, fulfilling experience. You see, soon, you'll have things inside you called hormones. And they'll make you do some pretty silly things. Like . . . attempted murder."

Neil takes a deep breath and closes his eyes for a second as if he's trying to suppress the words that are about to spill from his mouth.

"Ten years. Ten years of my life at Terminal Island. In a cage made for an animal. And you know what? That's what they turned me into. The system, their system, is fuckin' broken, man." Neil is taken by the memories now. There is no holding back his thoughts. He is completely engulfed by his confession.

"From the first day in that greasy, dank holding cell, I was fighting for my life. Trying to protect myself twenty-four fuckin' seven takes its toll, and I had to sleep. When I woke up, I was being . . . held down . . ." Neil grinds his teeth at the thought. He can't even speak of the things they did to him.

"I must have bought a ticket that day because they were runnin' train, man. Five of the biggest Mexicans I've ever seen. They raised their hands and blocked out my sun for a year. Every day was worse than the last. I was . . ." Trailing off, Neil winces, desperate to control his anger. He continues, "I was traded. Like a baseball card on a playground. Their 'little lady gringo' they said. Each time I was passed along, they'd brand me, sucking my soul a little drier every time. Some days, it's all I could do but lay in the infirmary, wishing there was a window I could look out of, just so I could see that the day was passing by. So I knew it wouldn't always be like this. I thought it was my darkest hour, but it was the night before the most brilliant fucking dawn and the last stop before I lost my humanity completely. 'What is it to be, man?' I'd think to myself during that time. I decided to answer that question one day in the yard.

"I was going to take a piece of myself back, and I caved one of those fucking Mexicans' skulls in with a twenty-pound weight. I remember it so clearly, it was like an orgasmic wave washing over my senses. I let it all go, and I became free. To be free, I had to become one of them." Neil smiles at the thought of his first kill. "I still remember the weight in my hand. It's kind of like a bowling ball. You remember, like that time when we bowled with Uncle Ron." Veronica giggles at the memory. She is far too young to grasp the moral complexities of Neil's story. He laughs, and continues.

"An Aryan front member by the name of Bill Cox saw my "work" in the yard that day. He allowed me to join his gang, a group of social misfits, hopped-up speed dealers, and violent trailer trash. White power assholes. That's when I got this." Neil unbuttons his shirt and reveals a faded, fist-sized tattoo of the Grim Reaper carrying a flag emblazoned with an iron cross.

"Veronica, I told you this was a goofy man in a coat, but it isn't. This is a symbol, a disgusting symbol of brotherhood and honour. One I had to get so I could be standing before you today. It's also the reason I can't come with you to the public pools. You think because you camped out one night behind the school for social studies, you know what survival is? Survival is this faded prison ink next to my heart." Neil buttons his shirt back up.

"The rest of my sentence, I spent with the Aryans. Seven years. Surviving. Every day, waking up and having to prove myself. If Bill pointed the finger, that person got—got. And I got a lot of people. Yeah, they asked me to kill, and every time I raised a pipe or a cheaply sharpened bed spring to someone, I was killing myself a little more. And I can't be punished for that. They can't extend your sentence for killing parts of your own soul; that's something I have to live with every day. Some people find God in jail, but I became one. Every morning, knowing that I would have to make a choice. If I felt like it, I could take a beating a little too far or just twist the blade when I put it in. Hispanics, Blacks, other Aryan members who were outta line, hell, even guards. I was so used to dancing on the edge that I became the fucking edge, and people just danced on me. Take a life; that's power. That is god." Neil rests a moment, taken aback by his own words.

"Three weeks before I was scheduled to get out, Bill said he would get some prison bitch to turn, to rat me out for all the shit I did so he could keep me inside. He told me that I was the next king after he bowed, and that I had to stay to help run until his reign was over. When I wouldn't agree, he grabbed me and told me that when he found me, I was a ball of clay, and because of him, I was hard. I knew then that if I didn't do something, I was gonna be shivved in the shower, bleeding out on the floor where I bled so many others.

The next day during our cushy prison back room kitchen duties, I stabbed him with a sharpened spoon. I nearly took his fuckin head off. I looked in his eyes as it went in, and I just saw black." Neil sighs hard. "But it was a reflection of myself. As I took away everything he'll ever have, every smile, every bit of fear, every month, every year, every day, every hour, every minute..." Neil trails off again. He shakes his head, trying to shake away the bad memory. The years of prison grime. The murders. He struggles to get back on track.

"I took it all from him, and I didn't even . . . I didn't even blink. I didn't even shutter. The last breath he took in was the one I expelled in my finest moment. The moment when the line in the sand between me and him disappeared." Neil stares blankly into the distance for a second trying to make sense of his thoughts. Trying to find some meaning in the haunting memories.

"Sometimes . . . sometimes in the night, I'll wake up. I can feel the warm blood spraying over my hands. I wash them endlessly, but they never come clean. Some people say they struggle with their history, but mine . . . mine has a fucking boot on my throat. And every day, I feel it pressing down harder and harder. My eyes well up with tears. My chest heaves, and the air becomes thin. It always eases up, but one day I don't think it will. And when that day comes, I will gladly burn in hell for the horrors of what I have done." Neil shuts his eyes, and his head drops to his chest. His confession hangs heavy in the silent, still room.

Like flipping a switch, Neil's head snaps up, and his fatherly demeanour returns. It's a complete 180 from how he was just a second ago; he's seemingly completely forgotten the ugly memories that had possessed him. He reaches for a banana and a condom that's sitting on the shelf of the easel.

"Anyways, this is a condom, and this banana will represent a penis."

FREDDY KRUEGER REMODELED MY KITCHEN

Maybe it was the kombucha at dinner, or maybe it was my son Rohan's everlasting spirit and love of play that tired me so, but by the time the philistines were discussing their "Sports Ball '' on the local news, I had dozed off. Usually, my dreams are congenial affairs of myself and Rohan activating our play centres in an endless field on a summer's day, but this was different. I dreamt that I was watching myself sleep in the chair in front of the TV when the TV slowly began to lift itself off of the ground. It had begun to grow legs. A boil-like head began to erupt from the top of the television. I noticed it was wearing a rather bedraggled fedora. I began to have my concerns; I'd heard of this phenomenon before. Once the arms began protruding from the sides and I got a look at the red and green striped sweater, I knew. Freddy Krueger had come to kill me. Half television, half-demented spirit, he stomped towards me.

Extending his razor-sharp fingers he exclaimed, "Isn't the news a scream!"

I'd heard of him before. Everyone in Springwood has. We had our reservations about moving here, but the price was right and outweighed by the slight chance of being murdered in our dreams. Wyntyr, my partner, had just birthed Rohan, and we needed to upgrade our living situation after the birthing pool leaked and ruined the floors of our downtown Austin loft.

"It's not like we're going to be living on Elm Street," Wyntyr argued. "Springwood is a big town, we'll probably never even bump into this Fredrick person."

And she was right, for a time, I suppose.

I narrowly ducked out of the way of his bladed glove as he swiped at me, making a fine mess of my August Beckett artisanal wicker chair. Even though he was awkward in his current form, he was still quick and I wasn't able to outmanoeuvre him. He grabbed my copy of Mark Z. Danielewski's House of Leaves off of a side table and hurled it at my head.

"This book is a real nightmare!" He cackled.

The impact put me in a daze and I stumbled back, tripping on Rohan's always-in-vogue set of wooden toys and finally through the drywall and onto the floor of the kitchen. Freddy, now looking like his usual self, wasn't done with me yet. He picked me up over his head and began banging me into the walls and cupboards, but with every impact I heard the sound of a pinball game. He pushed my head through the framed painting of Frida Kahlo wearing a Daft Punk shirt.

"Game over, asshole!" He yelled, tossing my limp body to the floor.

The kitchen, like myself, was destroyed. The walls were full of holes, the countertops smashed, and the few cabinet doors that still hung were stained with my blood. It was a total write-off.

Looming over top of me, Freddy admired the razor-sharp blades on his glove. “Your soul will give me strength. The strength I need to-” He stopped. I opened my eyes, slowly at first—almost too terrified of what I would see. Freddy was fixated on the wall in front of him. He walked towards it and tore off a piece of the loose drywall that he had bashed open with my face, exposing the beautiful brickwork underneath.

“Is this...natural brick?” he asked himself. “It is!” He began to look around the kitchen, studying the particulars. “This is a vaulted ceiling. If you got rid of these recessed lights and knocked it all out...you could have yourself a good space here.” Producing measuring tape out of his pocket, he began to measure the wall I had just crashed through. “Hmmm,” he murmured. “It has good bones.”

“This is your backsplash now, bitch!” Freddy Kruger yelled at Wyntyr. She didn’t even glance up from her June issue of Monocle. Freddy had been at it for more than two weeks now, and his presence had turned from anxiety-inducing to ordinary. We hadn’t seen any of the work he had done because large tarps covered both entrances to the kitchen. He kept surprisingly ordinary work hours for a supernatural being, always at around eight and leaving at five, lunch pail in hand.

Still, the lines of reality were blurring and I had to ask myself, “Am I in his nightmare, or is he in mine?”

There were certainly Freddy-like events going on: I'd hear creepy nursery rhymes floating in the wind, and there was a general feeling of unease in the house. But if he was controlling this world, would he really have had to recut that one piece of crown moulding so many times? Would he make so many trips to Home Depot? Couldn't Freddy just have the right amount of ceiling paint to finish the job?

Finally, the time came for the big unveiling. Freddy, unusually sheepish, tried to explain the concept but he quickly lost the words. Pulling back the tarp, I could see why.

Think "Venezuelan chop and chew," but not? "Industrial" vibe, but "French cottage feel"? I don't want to say "plantation-style" because of cancel culture, but I'll say plantation-style. But maybe it isn't any of those things. It was just...brilliant. And beautiful. And powerful. We adorned him with praise, but he was too humble, doffing his fedora, he inadvertently exposed his violently burnt brain to me.

"Maybe that's why his ideas are so scintillating," Wyntyr would later say, insisting that the fedora doff was a sign of affection, not unlike a common house cat flashing its belly. This man. This nightmare. This burnt child killer with a bladed leather glove had the mind for design, the passion for concepts and the peerless commitment to craftsmanship. He was an artist of the home.

Then the bill came.

Our life has been different since Freddy took Rohan as one of his dream warriors. The house seems to lack a bit of the life that it once had, but Wyntyr and I are both sleeping better than ever and the amount we've been able to declutter has been simply electric.

Whenever I give a tour of the house to someone new, more often than not they pause when they get to the kitchen. "I'd give my first born for a space like this," they say.

"Hey," I reply. "I know a guy."

CAMPING. JUST LIKE BEING AT HOME, BUT SHITTIER

Pulling up to my designated spot was like e-braking into heaven. Sure, my '97 Camry, loaded with every camping accessory I could get my grubby paws on, fought to get up that hill a few turns back, but it all seems worth it now. This is my escape from the real world. This is the ultimate adventure. Camping, just like being at home but shittier.

First up - my abode. 4x6 feet of absolute freedom. I pull out my double-walled blackout tent. I fumble with the poles and pegs and whatever else is in this confusing bag until a nice man in his 50s offers to help. I quickly offload the entire project of erecting the tent onto him. This is just like being at work - but shittier. After Frank (or maybe it was Gordon?) was finished setting up, I thanked him. He looked out of breath and frustrated, and I thought I should offer him water or something, but I'm just like my boss at home, but shittier.

The air mattress fills up brilliantly, and I collapse onto it. Just like my bed at home - but shittier. My back immediately begins to ache, and I get an awful cramp in my calf trying to get off it. Perfect. I love the setup time. It's like going back to a time when men built their houses with their bare hands, except that I bought all this awesome stuff from Walmart during that big sale at Christmas. “All camping accessories must go” indeed! Into the back of my car and then into my stank basement for months and months. I laugh at the memory and flick a crushed-up dead spider off the mattress. Just like my bed at home but shittier.

I’ve worked up quite the sweat setting all this stuff up, time to hit the public showers. Turning on the water, opening up that squeaky valve, the water begins to surge. Propelled by a shower head akin to a pressure washer, the field of spray is reduced down to a single point of pressure and it leaves ugly red marks on my chest and anywhere else on my body that is unfortunate enough to be lashed by its unforgiving strength. The water is so hard, so chock-full of minerals that no matter how hard I try, I cannot get the soap to lather. God, I love this stuff. Just like the shower at home, but shittier.

Walking back to the campsite, I take a look at all the normies in their huge trailers and gigantic 4x4 trucks. They don’t get it. These trailers are far nicer than my studio apartment, and that’s not the point of camping. It’s supposed to be worse than home; that’s the whole idea. Hell, maybe these normies' houses are worse than their $80,000 trailers and RVs. Woah, did I just gain the ability to empathize? That’s the power of nature. It’s wild. This is just like therapy at home, but shittier.

I’m getting a bit hungry, so it’s time to set up the kitchen. I hang my fully stocked spice rack from the tree near my predetermined eating area, where it is immediately attacked by a number of furious critters. I next spend a good deal of time assembling the butane double-burner stove along with its matching grill and pizza oven accessory. The whole apparatus is supported by two flimsy legs that have no hope of standing on this uneven terrain. This is my kitchen. Just like the one at home, but shittier.

I notice a young woman across from me at the next campsite, dressed in white. She wears a mournful look on her face. In front of her on the picnic table, she writes in a beat-up notebook, poetry no doubt. We share eye contact for a second before she returns to her process. Just like Sylvia Plath at home, but shittier.

I throw my mouthwatering New York strip sirloin on the side burner, but the whole kitchen apparatus tips from the weight. Seeing dollar signs go down the toilet, my instincts kick in, and I reach to stop the momentum, but alas, for my troubles, I receive only a dirt-covered steak, a destroyed kitchen unit, and a deep, deep cut on the inside of my palm. Later, as I was bleeding heavily into the sink, my dirty open wound struck a fellow camper's attention. "You should get that looked at," he mentions, concerned. Just like medical advice at home, but shittier.

Lying in the tent, sweating profusely, the infection running deeper and deeper into my body, my Apple Watch goes off with alerts from Insta. "Fuck yeah buddy, that's a picture of a tree," I think to myself when I see that my friend Kurtis has liked the picture of a tree that I took. That guy has never specifically even suggested that he enjoys trees, so this is big. I feel the chills, light-headedness, and fever run through my body. This is just like the initial stages of sepsis at home, but shittier.

Later, I'm shaken awake by the momentum of the ambulance weaving through the campground roads with some haste. The man above me shines a light into my eyes. He looks with disgust at the severely infected wound on my hand and my rapidly dropping blood pressure. In and out of consciousness now, I think back to my camping adventure. The drive-in, the first smell of the trees, Garry or whatever his name was being out of breath after setting up my tent, the last day or so of hallucinations brought on from the swelling of my blood-brain barrier. "I can't wait for next summer," I whisper over and over to myself as a thin man, faceless and dressed in black, impossibly slides his way through the crack of the ambulance doors. He begins at my feet, and his massive jaws slowly work their way up, swallowing me whole into the forever blackness. The grim clutches of death that await every person who takes even a single breath in this life just like at home, but shittier.

I AM A CONDUCTOR AND I HAVE NO IDEA WHAT I'M DOING

Life is a funny thing sometimes. One day you're wandering the streets, unemployed and unemployable, when all at once you're surrounded by wasps. You swat at them, your arms gesturing wildly in the air, trying to protect both your face and the open can of Dr. Pepper that is in your pocket. This goes on for some time, unfortunately. Or...fortunately? The incredibly brave act of fighting off these wasps, of standing your ground and not giving them the can of Dr. Pepper as they demand shifts the universe in a fundamental way. For once things are moving in your direction, instead of constantly pulling away from you. The wasps disperse, the battle over for now. A human hand slaps you hard on the shoulder and says, “Son, that's the best goddamn conducting I've ever seen.” Within an hour you have a six-figure salary, a fancy little stick and all the Dr. Pepper you can drink.

That was me. That was my story. In the 20 years since, I have travelled the world, performed for dignitaries and royalty, bought a bread maker and made my own brioche and I'm not ashamed to say that I have no clue what I'm doing when it comes to conducting an orchestra. It used to bother me, but nowadays I couldn't care less. Standing in front of a hundred musicians with their various thing-a-ma-jigs (I could never be bothered to learn the names of the musical contraptions that they waste their lives learning) I just tap my fancy stick on the paper holder to get everyone to stop screwing around, hold my arms in the air for a moment and when I bring them down everyone starts playing. Bing bang boom. "Gesticulate and eat the cake," as we conductors say. And guess what? I'm not alone. Most conductors I know have no idea what they are doing either.

But why would we? What do we actually do? I mean, the musicians, as much as they are an absolute pain in my ass, know the songs well enough on their own, and if they don't, they have sheet music sitting in front of them. And from what I'm told there is a hell of a lot more information on those pages than what I could possibly impart to them with my fancy stick thingy in the middle of a performance for the Queen and her ring of pedophiles. I'm essentially a hype man for a royalty-free cover band and I have zero problems with it.

The best part of the job is the annual conductor conventions. Our drug-fuelled parties would make Hunter S. Thompson look like the conformist normie that he probably was. We, conductors, hold these conventions for what we call the three G's: Gettin' high, Gettin' drunk, and Gettin' money. I once walked into a conference room and what I saw put an honest to God white streak in my hair, as if I'd seen a troubling vision from the "other side." Quite frankly, I think I did. My fancy little stick can't wait until next year. That's a bit of conductor humour for you. BTW, none of us know what the stick is called.

Once in a while, you run into some keener at a convention who actually knows what they are doing and it is a huge bummer. They are usually passionate and talkative about things like Allegros and Concertos and god knows what else. It takes everything in me not to tell them that I'm just trying to haul as much shrimp into this sinking vessel as I can before all the fans of this music die off and I can no longer afford to cycle in a brand new leather sectional in my living room every three years. But the good news is that there are a lot more of us that are ignorant of our duties than there are competent ones, so we've managed to keep this trade secret pretty hush-hush.

Because, sadly, it's true. Time is running out on us. The younger generation doesn't understand classical music. They don't think music should be "boring" or a "chore to listen to," and I get it. We're not exactly Mick Jagger up there, mincing around and flashing everyone our horny lips. People have grown disinterested in this old woody music that we play and I cannot afford to be ignorant any longer. So I've taken up a new profession, one that is actually less work and requires less knowledge than being a conductor. I've become a DJ. I don't get paid as much (yet) but there are no dry cleaning bills and I get to hang out with a younger crowd. Most every night is like the conductor conventions of old, and my hair is now completely white from bursting into so many rooms and seeing so many horrible, sexy things.

I do miss it though; the power, the prestige. The roar of the orchestra when those guys with the things pounded on those drum things, and the people with the tiny shoulder guitars went all high at the end of the song. And who could forget the blowers, blowing into those tin things? Incredible. There is truly nothing like it.

BATHROOM BUDDIES

MONDAY 9:07 AM

Alex pushes open the door and makes his way into the small, stuffy bathroom. He stops to check his appearance in the mirror, and he is let down by what is reflected back at him; his young, peckish face has grown old in recent months. He didn't get much sleep the night before, and he's feeling the effects this morning. It shows on his face. The bags under his eyes hold bloodshot marbles that give him the appearance of an older man, but he's still in his mid-twenties. The bathroom itself is a typical auxiliary office bathroom: two urinals compressed into a four-foot space between the stall and sink, offering little in the way of privacy. Shrugging his body off of the counter in front of the sink, he moves to the urinal closest to the stall, unzips his pants, and begins his business of urination. With great flourish, the bathroom door swings open and Nathan comes rushing in. He quickly moves past Alex and into the private stall, and after a moment, he unleashes a powerful torrent of urine. The harsh sound bounces off of the bare walls of the room.

“How’s it going, Alex?” Nathan asks, having to speak up to be heard over the raging piss.

He stares at the wall inches in front of his face. He doesn’t want to engage in conversation at this exact moment. He instead quickly finishes up and begins to do up his pants.

“I’m alright, I guess. Jarvis is on my ass about these Malaysian manufacturing problems,” Alex responds. He turns on the sink and begins to wash his hands. Nathan rips open the stall door with a flourish and moves close to Alex, checking himself out in the mirror. His smug appearance is in perfect contrast to Alex’s drabness. Like some kind of miracle before and after drug advertisement photo.

“I know that game, buddy.” Nathan checks his teeth in the mirror and picks out a small piece of pepper between his front teeth. He slaps Alex on the back. “Fuckin’ Jarvis, amirite?”

Lost in the act of washing his hands, Alex doesn’t respond. Nathan slaps him on the back again.

“I gotta get back out there. See ya later, ya prick!” Nathan exclaims as he leaves the bathroom without washing his hands.

Alex lets the cool water run over his hands for another minute.

MONDAY 3:39 PM

He had just begun urinating at the same urinal beside the private stall. Alex, still stuck in his foul mood, wears it unabashedly on his face. Nathan launches into the bathroom in a rush, but his stride slows as he sees Alex at the urinal. He continues into the private stall.

"Jesus, Alex, we're like 'bathroom buddies' or something," Nathan says, laughing at the situation.

Alex laughs, and his bad mood lifts for a moment.

"Hey, great dicks think alike."

"Too true," Nathan says back, now urinating loudly.

Alex finishes up and begins washing his hands in the sink. His mood has lightened considerably. He looks at his face in the mirror as he washes his hands and shrugs off the tired look.

"Bathroom buddies, that's precious," Alex says, half to himself.

Nathan calls out from the private stall, "What was that?"

Alex is a little embarrassed that he has almost been caught being so cheerful by a stupid, off-handed connection.

"Nothing . . . nothing." He dries his hands and walks out of the bathroom.

TUESDAY 9:02 AM

Strolling into the bathroom, Alex's face carries the look of expectation. Like a schoolboy with a crush waiting at a bus stop, his mood is a complete one-eighty from the funk he was in the day before. His clothes are pressed and nice, emulating Nathan's everyday look: smart, casual, and confident. But the bathroom is empty and hauntingly still. Alex checks the private stall, and his good mood seems to evaporate into anxious worry. He walks to the urinal and begins to undo his pants. There is no familiar sound of urination and after several seconds Alex looks back at the closed bathroom door. Several moments pass with no sound. Slowly Alex reaches out his hand and caresses the wall of the private stall, and finally, the sound of urination fills the room.

WEDNESDAY 9:18 AM

Nathan cheerily walks into the bathroom and stops short when he sees Alex standing ominously in front of the stall door. Alex is dishevelled. He still wears the clothes he had on yesterday, but now they are wrinkled with the wear of the day and possibly an entire night. He has been there. Waiting. Waiting for Nathan. Waiting for his bathroom buddy.

Stuck in midstep, Nathan is so unsettled he briefly considers turning around and leaving the bathroom. Against his better judgement, he slowly walks around Alex and towards the private stall. The bathroom is cramped, awkward, and silent. Nathan feels compelled to say something . . . anything to break the tension.

"Hey, man . . . h-how's it going?" stumbles out of Nathan's mouth.

Alex says nothing, his face fixed in a dead, expressionless stare. The only indication that he is not catatonic is that his eyes follow Nathan across the room. Nathan makes his way to the stall and locks the door. The room is silent, save for Alex's increasingly audible breathing and Nathan unfastening his belt. The silence is broken by Nathan's sudden stream of urination. Alex says something, but Nathan can't quite make out what it is.

"What did you say?" he asks, but there is no response. He pushes out his urine with every ounce of strength in his body, the resulting stream is more powerful than anything Nathan has ever unleashed in his life. His knees shake, and his urethral sphincters squeeze to free the piss with as much force as possible. With his pants only half done up, he unlocks the stall door and opens it to find that Alex is gone. What was it that he overheard? It sounded like: I know about him.

WEDNESDAY 3:27 PM

Alex walks into the bathroom. He's even more dishevelled than he was the last time we saw him. He sluggishly walks to the urinal beside the private stall, unzips his pants, and lets out a loud sigh. There is no sound of urination. After a few long moments, Alex violently punches the wall of the private stall.

WEDNESDAY 3:39 PM

The hallway outside of the bathroom is calm and practically deserted. At the far end, Alex anxiously peers around the corner where he has a direct line of sight to the bathroom, their bathroom. Uncomfortable, he repositions himself, and in doing so leaves a large, wet handprint of sweat on the dull beige wall. His eyes widen like a hunter catching first sight of his prey; Nathan and another man walk in step with each other down the hallway. The man Nathan is with is about Alex's age but obviously more good-looking, like an "upgraded Alex." He confidently gestures with his hand while he speaks, and the men laugh loudly together. Alex swallows hard to contain his anger, but tears well up in his eyes as Nathan holds the bathroom door open and "upgraded Alex" walks through.

WEDNESDAY 10:35 PM

His posture perfect, Alex sits up against the headboard in bed. His arms are crossed, his leg shakes, and he has chewed his lip bloody red. Alex's wife, Marissa, lies beside him. She reads on an iPad.

"I don't want to have sex with you," he says, seemingly out of nowhere.

Alex quickly rolls over on his side, pulls the blankets tight around himself and shuts his bedside light off. Marissa is speechless and confused.

"Wha . . .?" She asks, the word not even fully forming before leaving her mouth.

Alex doesn't respond.

THURSDAY 9:45 AM

Carefully sticking his head into the bathroom, Nathan takes a look around. He lets out a sigh of relief; the bathroom is empty. He pushes the rest of his body through the small crack he made for his head as if opening the door all the way would draw some sort of alarm. He stops once he is a few steps into the bathroom as he notices the private stall door is closed. Cautiously, Nathan makes his way to the door of the stall and pushes it open.

Inside the stall is an abundance of gifts. Sweaters and new ties hang from the walls, and the toilet tank has a few lavishly decorated gift bags on it. Poking around the gift bags, he finds a handmade card. On the cover of the card is a drawing of a toilet paper roll and an empty toilet paper dispenser. He opens the card and inside the words "Only You" are scrawled in large red letters.

FRIDAY 9:10 AM

Alex is sitting on the counter of the bathroom, looking cool and relaxed as Nathan sheepishly walks in. It takes a moment that feels like forever, but Nathan eventually looks up from the ground to make eye contact. Alex's steely look excites Nathan in a way that he hasn't felt in a long time. Alex gestures towards the private stall. Nathan subtly nods and makes his way in. Alex hops up from the counter and walks to his urinal. The sound of the fluorescent lights and the hum of the overhead fan—have all disappeared now, replaced by the deafening noise of expectation.

"I'm glad you came," Alex says confidently.

"Me too," Nathan softly replies.

Alex's forwardness and businesslike tone make the hair on Nathan's neck stand up.

"Thank you for the gifts."

"It's no problem. I haven't felt like spoiling someone like that in a long time," Alex says. There is a long moment of silence.

"I'm looking forward to the Eurythmics box set," Nathan says sheepishly.

"I knew you would like it . . . buddy?" The words leave Alex's mouth more like a question than a statement. Nathan takes a deep breath.

"I do . . . buddy."

Alex reaches out his hand and begins to slowly caress the wall of the private stall. Nathan, on the other side of the wall, begins to do the same. The slow, elegant moves of their hands mimic each other perfectly, almost as if they share the same mind. Soon, the moves evolve and become more extravagant, like a hostile ballet or a Chinese ribbon dance. Both men's arms glide over the smooth surface of the stall. They move unashamed, urine confidently spraying into their respective dockers. They move. As one.

"What the hell are you two assholes doing?" The man's loud voice bounces around the empty bathroom. Jarvis, Alex and Nathan's previously unseen boss, now stands in the middle of the bathroom. He's too angry that they're not at work to realize the full extent of what was going on. Alex and Nathan struggle to compose themselves.

"I swear to god, this whole office spends more time fucking around in the bathroom than sitting at their goddamn desks doing their fucking jobs!" Jarvis screams at them.

Nathan squeezes past Jarvis and runs out of the room, embarrassed and ashamed. Alex calls out after him, but it's clear he's never coming back. They are bathroom buddies no more.

YOU'RE A MILLENNIAL, BUY A CASKET

So, you're buying a casket. Good for you. Buying a casket changed my life and I'm a lot like you: 30-ish, disillusioned, just got out of a stick-and-poke tattoo phase, and always searching for some sense of security in this scary world. It may not seem like it, but I can guarantee you that buying a casket is the only sound financial decision you will ever make.

I know what you're thinking. "I'm just going to rot in it, what do I need all the bells and whistles for?" I have two words for you: Content Creation. Death is everywhere: TikTok, Instagram, it trends on X everyday.

Imagine the views on your reel of you posing beside your solid copper casket, the flood of comments informing you of your "dope decision" and how "gangster" you will be once you are dead. This is your chance to become an influencer. #casketlife

Today you're at home, probably watching The Office, thinking that micro-dosing psilocybin mushrooms will magically change your life. But, buy that coffin, and tomorrow you could be whisked away on an all-expenses-paid trip to be measured by the coolest undertaker DJs and attending parties at the sexiest cemeteries in Berlin. The free gifts: casket linings, hinge upgrades, corpse pillows and more will flood your house on the reg. The grave bell is the new freak flag—let yours fly, baby.

Yes. The cost. About that. It may shock you. Your casket will cost you more than the car you currently drive. I won't sugarcoat it, this casket will be the most expensive thing you will ever own.

But I have some tips. Once the payment clears, the casket is yours to do what you want with. Take it home and USE the damn thing. Having people over for a BBQ? Fill it with ice, toss some beers in it and you have a great-looking cooler. Put your TV on it and it becomes an art deco media centre. Halloween accessory? Check. Unsettling Christmas decoration that reminds your parents of their fragile mortality? Check.

"But I can get a coffin for much cheaper," you might say. A coffin? Ew. What are you some Eurotrash vampire? Marylin Manson has a stack of them on his lawn next to a sign marked "Free," and you want to buy one? For once in your life, sort that price list from high to low. Don't cheap out on this. You will never, ever be able to afford a house, let alone a nice one so you might as well splurge on your eternal resting place.

Real talk? Get a credit card, make the minimum payments and just, you know, maybe you won't have to pay the whole balance off. I don't mean to be morbid but you really never know what can happen and lately you have been eating like shit.

Minimalism is something we tell ourselves that we desire because we can't afford the life our parents had the privilege to lead. What is more minimalist than living in your own casket? If Apple could design a home, it would have the elegant, clean lines and colour scheme of the inside of the casket you are buying today. Face it, rent is never going to go down, it will only keep rising and one day you won't have a choice. Picture it with me: after a typical eight to twelve hour workday at your open-concept-sweatshop-chic marketing job, you will tell yourself that food is an experience as you eat a gas station sandwich for dinner, arriving just after dark to the embankment under a bridge where your casket has been painstakingly camouflaged with garbage to keep intruders from shitting in it. Crack open the lid and you are home. Rent-free. Mortgage-free. "Why aren't more people doing this?" You'll ask yourself as the lack of oxygen puts you into a woozy slumber.

The time will come when it will be up to the millennials to shape this world how we see fit. From the economy, to politics, to commerce there is a long road ahead of us to unfuck the world. We will wake up refreshed from a good night's sleep in our caskets and emerge from under our bridges to face the challenges of this world. So what are you waiting for? Buy a casket already.

A PREVIEW OF THE HOME DEPOT STREAMING SERVICES ORIGINAL CONTENT

Move over Netflix, move over Disney+; there is a new player in stream town, and it smells like fresh-cut wood and daily tool rentals. Home Depot+ is going live later this month, and their cart is overflowing with big-name talent. I got a preview of the new streaming platform's first foray into original content. Here is what you can expect to binge in the near future.

Bob Vila: Nazi Hunter

Bob Vila is back, but he's done fixing old houses; he's fixing the errors of the Nuremberg trials. This reality show combines aspects of history and travel TV into a winning formula. Vila travels hot on the heels of war criminals through exotic locals such as Brazil, Argentina, and Alberta. Following leads, historical evidence, and word of mouth, Bob is joined by a young, sexy group of experts to help him on his way. His amazing chemistry with Abigail Wyterfyll, his gadget expert, is something to keep your eye on. Their banter while she navigates the Home Depot app is the real star of the show. This isn't a slow burn either, as Bob catches a Nazi at the end of every episode. No spoilers, but you've never seen entertainment until you've seen Bob Vila use a RYOBI 2,300 PSI High-Performance Electric Pressure Washer on the screaming face of a 95-year-old Nazi.

But you know Bob; just because he's hunting Nazis doesn't mean there isn't time to frame an addition onto a house or help better insulate a few old windows along the way.

Bevelled Edge

You want big names? Home Depot+ has plenty in stock, but the biggest might be the master of prestige TV: Sopranos creator David Chase. He returns to create and show-run "Bevelled Edge," a slick update of the material that made him the most wanted creative mind in television. Dennis Franz plays Lester Harringwood, a newly hired employee at Home Depot. Seemingly an ordinary retiree seeking extra income at a great job with great benefits, Lester's hidden past is slowly catching up with him. The master of pace, Chase lets us meditate on long shots of Franz's character as he watches Home Depot new hire training videos about important policies and customer wellness. The season hits its stride in episode two with a 25-minute dream sequence featuring detailed instructions on how to integrate the Home Depot app into your Nest system. Already renewed for season two, James Woods will join the cast as Jimmy Birch, a garden centre employee who loves his great job at Home Depot. Could this be the start of the Home Depot Cinematic Universe?

As a bonus, finishing the first season of “Bevelled Edge” automatically fulfills a day of new hire training at any Home Depot location in the continental United States.

Trans-Atlantic

After a freak hurricane levels the fictional town of Barsenwood, Maine, a father reaches out to his estranged son to help rebuild the family home. Having been displaced himself in Manhattan, the son accepts the offer and shows up on the father’s doorstep, but *record scratch,* He is now transitioning to be a woman. The father is an ol’ fashioned guy and let’s just say he’s more than a little shocked at this turn of events. What this dramedy lacks in star power, it makes up for in the exploration of the relationship between fathers and daughters, new beginnings, and how the Home Depot app can be used not just for shopping but also as a helpful tool for builders young and old, trans or cis, liberal or Republican.

Sexuality, trans rights, tips on countertop installation? Are you sure this is Home Depot+? You’re damn right it is.

Red, White and Orange

September 11th, 2001 changed America, and the world, in countless ways. In this six part series, we follow director Alex Gibney as he renovates his brand-new Manhattan loft and interviews contractors, day labourers and the occasional helpful Home Depot employee that he meets along the way about their feelings about 9/11 now and then.

Should we have started the war on terror? What did we gain when we lost our privacy? Which blade should you use to cut a glass backsplash with? Part true crime, part investigative journalism, part home reno adventure on a budget, Red, White and Orange will leave you asking, “What did we lose when the brothers fell?” *Insert contractually obliged reference to the Home Depot app*

Right out of the gate, Home Depot+ is reno-ing the new media landscape with their lineup of original content. With recent production deals with Conan O’Brien and David Simon, Home Depot is positioning itself to be a streaming monster, unafraid to tackle race, sexuality and what it means to be human in this day and age. With the licensing deals to exclusively stream Home Improvement, House Hunters International and Oz, I have a feeling you’ll be bingeing Home Depot+ with one hand and browsing the excellent Home Depot app with the other. Happy bingeing!

ESCALATING PAGEANTRY

It is three hours until showtime at the Samantha Martin Memorial Curling Rink. Today, the ice has been covered, and the stones and the brooms have been stowed away in order to make room for tonight's event: "IHHF's Ballzout Wrestling," the monthly independent wrestling show.

Adam and Russell stand in line at the canteen in the midst of one of their many discussions about how to get ahead in the wrestling business. Both men, far into their mid-30s, are not exactly what you would see on a polished TV product; neither is technically out of shape, but they certainly lack the chiselled physique that dominates the "big time" wrestling world. In their street clothes, they could be confused for audience members.

"Two words, my friend: Escalating Pageantry," Adam tells Russell with great confidence in his voice.

"I have no idea what that means," Russell replies.

Adam is not shaken in the least.

"Escalating pageantry," he repeats, slower and more deliberately.

Between the two, Adam could be considered the "veteran," having wrestled exactly one more time than Russell has.

"I know the phrase, but I don't see how it helps us right now," Russell tells Adam, who is growing impatient with explaining himself.

"Here, let me see your phone," Adam tells Russell.

"Okay, but be careful. I'm almost out of minutes," Russell says as he digs his phone out of his pocket and hands it to Adam. As he begins to google some kind of explanation, Nick, another mid-30s wrestling wannabe and also Adam's cousin, approaches the men in line with a shocked look on his face.

"Hey, Nick, what's wrong?" Russell asks. A little dazed, Nick takes a moment to reply.

"I just . . . got fired." He finally responds.

Russell goes in for a hug. He wraps his arms around Nick, who absolutely hates this more than anything in the universe. His arms hang draped over Russell's, which are wrapped tightly around his torso. It looks more like a reverse fireman's carry than a friendly embrace.

"You never struck me as someone who could be, you know, employed," Adam says without looking up from the phone in his hand.

Russell's hug still lingers. Nick grows increasingly uncomfortable with every passing moment.

"It's okay, buddy," Russell says gently into his ear.

"So were you like . . . a garbage man? Or a drug dealer?" Adam asks.

Nick finally pushes Russell off of him.

"Get off of me, you fucking freak," he says, more exhausted than angry. Nick adjusts himself for a second, trying to find some dignity. "I was an elementary school teacher."

Russell and Adam look shocked.

"Really?" Adam asks.

"Really?" Russell adds.

"Really?" Adam repeats again.

"Yes. Really. I'm good with children. And I take offence that you thought I was a drug dealer," Nick snaps at Adam.

"Well, to be fair, you used to sell us drugs," Russell says, defending Adam.

"Well, that was a long time ago. It looks like this is my full-time job now," Nick sighs as the words leave his mouth.

Adam and Russell collectively release a sound akin to a "woof" from their mouths. There is silence between the three men for a moment.

"I made eight dollars last week," Russell says. Nick and Adam release their own, quieter collective "woof".

"What were you going to show me?" Russell asks Adam, who still holds his phone.

"Oh, just this," Adam replies, handing the phone back to Russell. He looks at it and is shocked to see a picture of a man, or at least what is left of him, that has been hit by a train.

"Oh man, come on," Russell says.

Nick laughs, knowing what is going on. He grabs the phone out of Russell's hand to see the photo.

"Classic Adam, never give this guy your phone. It's always dead bodies with this guy."

Nick and Adam chuckle while Russell attempts to unsee the horrible picture, which, of course, is impossible.

"What are you going to do for money?" Adam asks Nick.

"Well, let's just say an old friend is coming back to town," Nick replies in a mysterious way.

"That sounds, uh, mysterious," Adam adds.

"Don't worry buddy, tonight your perogies are on me," Russell says reassuringly to Nick as he wraps his arm around his shoulder, which in turn makes Nick wince.

"ROSIE! TWO PLATES OF PEROGIES AND MAKE 'EM WET!" Russell yells into the window of the canteen.

Rosie, the canteen operator, slops a ladle of hot murky perogie water onto a plate of cold, congealed perogies. A smile crosses her face.

"Nobody makes it wet like Rosie," she muses to herself. A wheezing breath escapes her mouth before a smoker's cough acts up and she begins to violently hack all over her kitchen utensils.

The half-assembled ring stands in the middle of the mostly empty curling rink. It's only by the grace of the hillbilly gods that the ring doesn't collapse at every event. Two teenagers begin mounting the ropes to complete the ring. They squabble about how to tighten the ropes before they are both chastised by a veteran wrestler. This is a common right of passage; before you get to be in the ring, you have to learn how to set it up. Sometimes it takes a year before you even get to try out for an independent wrestling promotion. Every spot is earned. None are given. It is two hours until showtime.

Adam wears a feather boa. He shows it off to Russell in different ways.

"You keep saying it, but I don't know what it means," Russell says, confused.

Around them, in the makeshift locker room, are various other wrestlers on the card that night. The group of men runs the gamut of costumes and gimmicks: a sizeable amount of cowboys (owing to the prairie setting and how it is an easy costume to accomplish because you just need a pair of jeans), a deranged clown, a pretty boy, and even a few veteran workers who have had brushes with the big time, but plenty more who have never brushed against anything other than an underage girl.

Being relatively new to the wrestling promotion, Adam, Russell, and Nick have the worst-positioned stalls out of everyone: right beside the toilet. Rosie's Canteen giveth and Rosie's Canteen taketh away. The smell of some 20-odd wrestlers and their various strange hangers-on is a constant reminder of where Russell and Adam's wrestling career is in the big picture of the wrestling business.

Russell finishes putting on his royal blue singlet, a symbol of his "everyman" persona. Adam has recently switched his gimmick (yet again) to a grunge-type character. He comes out in a plaid shirt, baggy ripped jeans revealing long underwear underneath The outfit is complimented with sunglasses and a purple bass guitar.

"I think I'm gonna change up the gimmick," Adam casually says as he buttons up his plaid shirt. Russell sighs.

"Every time. You say that every time we get ready."

"It's not working!"

"Well, you're not getting booed anymore. Not like when you were," Russell grimaces as the words leave his mouth, "Sugar Tits Terry."

Adam laughs. "Yeah, who would have thought my transgender character would be such a flop? I did get on all those blogs, though. Who would have thought the scum that come to our shows would be so 'woke'?"

"I mean, I got it. It was a tribute."

"Damn right," Adam says with much bravado, pulling a guitar tuner out of his locker.

"I don't think the bass has to be in tune . . .?" Russell asks, staring at Adam as he connects the bass to the tuner.

"Kayfabe baby. Live the gimmick," Adam replies.

Kurtis, tonight's and, well, every night's referee, barges into the locker room directly in between Russell and Adam. A born-again Christian and the owner's brother-in-law, he had weaselled his way into being the referee because, literally, no one else wanted to do the job. Nick—and by proxy, Adam and Russell—has never gotten along with Kurtis. Nick claims it's because they had gone to school together, and Nick had dosed Kurtis with "magic" mushrooms in the eleventh grade. He then proceeded to lock Kurtis in the trunk of a car for two hours. When the locksmith finally got the trunk open, Kurtis had shit himself. If you ask this narrator, and you didn't, that's a pretty good basis for a lifelong feud.

"Have you guys seen Nick? I heard he has a friend coming in from out of town that I would love to meet." Kurtis rubs his hands together in a fittingly rat-like way.

"No, we haven't seen him in a few days," Russell says. "Anyways, I—"

Russell is interrupted by Kurtis.

"Too bad. I'm supposed to meet a friend of his."

He stands there for a moment his finger in the air, waiting for Russell and Adam to inquire further into the comment. The men look at each other and to the floor, hoping Kurtis will just get the point and leave.

"A fri—" Before Kurtis can get 'friend' out of his mouth, Adam interrupts him.

"Jesus Christ, shut up. No one likes you. Will you please, please, please fuck off?"

Kurtis is miffed at this little outburst.

"You know, you guys, you bottom-rung fecking hangin'-out-by-the-toilet nobodies, are so close to being poop-canned off this promotion it's not even funny. You know who the friend of Nick's I want to meet is? Drugs. He's selling drugs to everyone in this goshdarn locker room, and as soon as I catch him, I'm talking to Owner Doug and Continuous John, and ALL of you fecking clowns are getting thrown out of this locker room, and we'll all be better for it."

Adam and Russell stare at Kurtis as he finishes his rant.

"What do you think about that?"

"You know," Adam says, looking at the ceiling like he is trying to recall some piece of information, "I always thought you shit your pants in that trunk, but it smells like you shit out of your mouth."

Adam and Russell both laugh. Kurtis looks pissed. He continues to rant at them about Nick and "poop canning" them while walking back towards the door of the locker room. It's all meant to be threatening but quickly turns into absurdity as Kurtis blindly steps into a large, shallow pot of chilli that is cooling on the floor.

"Darnit, Harrison!" Kurtis yells to the other side of the locker room. "No more darn chilli in the locker room!" Hopping on one chilli-free leg, he leaves in an angry huff.

Nick bursts out of the locker beside Adam and Russell. He is out of breath.They look at him, confused. As his eyes adjust to the light, he notices Adam's feather boa.

"Nice. Escalating Pageantry," Nick says without missing a beat. "That's a good way to get ahead."

"Nick, are you selling drugs?" Russell asks, concerned.

"No, Russell, I'm not selling drugs," Nick answers back in a condescending manner, like a child talking to his mother.

"Good," Russell replies.

"Because I sold them all already. Look at this!" Nick pulls out a wad of bills. Russell doesn't look impressed.

"Who'd you sell drugs to?"

Nick gives Russell a 'who the fuck do you think' look and gestures to the breadth of the locker room.

"This is an independent wrestling show, Russell. Grow a fucking brain."

Russell shrugs. He's naive, yes, but no one should be that naive.

"How long were you in that locker for?" Adam finally asks. "We've been in this room for like 45 minutes."

"Who knows, man? I've been tripping balls for hours."

"Tripping? Tripping on what?"

"Acid."

"You sold acid to everyone wrestling tonight?" Russell asks.

"The Chilli Dogger cleaned out the stash. But yeah, the wrestlers and the managers. And the promoter. And the promoter's son. And the ring staff. And the towel boys. And Rosie from the canteen. And Jerry, the janitor. And the refs. Except for Kurtis, fuck that clown."

"How much did you take?" Adam inquires for shits and giggles.

"Probably like . . . hmmm . . ." Nick wonders for a moment. "Like . . . fourteen hits."

Adam and Russell just stare at Nick.

"Well, I've been doing it all day."

T-shirts, DVDs and cheap Chinese-made "swag" cover the walls of the hastily erected merchandise booths that fill the lobby in the Samantha Martin Memorial Curling Rink. It's a twisted carnival of overpriced wares that every wrestling spectator must make it through to gain entrance to this evening's show. It is one hour to showtime.

Adam lies on the floor of the changing room stretching while Nick rubs himself judiciously in cooking oil. Adam sits up and begins to stare at his hands.

"I don't think this acid is working," he remarks to Nick.

"Well, maybe if you would stop stretching like some kind of pussy it would work."

"Mr. Nick! Mr. Nick!" a child's voice calls out.

Nick tenses up and looks around for the source of the voice. A young boy around age eleven with a VIP pass is running towards them.

"What kind of parent lets their kids watch this shit? Let alone get them a VIP pass," Adam asks Nick, who isn't listening to him.

"Shit. That's one of the kids I teach. Or I used to teach anyway."

Nick turns and tries to busy himself in the locker, but it is far too late. Adam is confused.

"When you said 'teacher,' I thought you meant you were a garbage man that teaches other garbage men how to be garbage men."

The little boy runs up to the two men. Nick is dripping with cooking oil, and Adam is pretty sure the acid is beginning to kick in.

"Wow, you look like a bit of an asshole, huh?" the boy says, his eyes darting between Adam and Nick. The kid isn't wrong, but he doesn't have to say it like that. Nick is humiliated to be seen like this, and Adam is just kind of high.

"It's just a . . . uh . . . a bit of fun," Nick responds while the embarrassment of the universe engulfs him.

"Can I get a picture?" the boy asks, handing his phone to Adam.

"No, you see, that would be breaking kayfabe, and I really can't—"

The boy is not listening to Nick's complex explanation of subtleties of the wrestling world. He positions himself beside Nick and flexes his nonexistent Bicep. Nick gives in and unenthusiastically does the same hoping this will be over sooner if he complies.

"I can't believe this! What a bunch of fucking looooosers!" the boy yells into Nick's ear.

Adam fumbles with the phone for a second before turning it sideways to take a picture.

"Horizontal, jackass, it's for the gram! I've got 1200 followers, and I don't want some moron screwing this up," the boy yells at Adam, who sighs. This child is ruining his high.

"Alright, on the count of three, say 'Garbageman!'" Adam instructs his subjects.

"One, two, three!"

The boy enthusiastically yells 'Garbageman' while Nick lazily mumbles 'Fuck you' in a perverse unison.

The excited boy grabs the phone from Adam to look at the picture. To his surprise, the photo on his phone is a gruesome picture of a man who has been electrocuted.

"What the . . ."

"Why don't you run along and . . . uhh . . . fuck off somewhere else," Adam says dismissively to the now disturbed child.

Sullen-faced, he slowly makes his way out of the locker room, stripped of his childhood innocence. Nick gives Adam a 'look.' Adam shrugs his shoulders.

"It's what I do."

The crowd is sparse but lively tonight. They sit on metal folding chairs. Some eat, some sit with their elbows on their knees, their heads resting in the palms of their hands. Some are attending ironically—enticed by the garish spectacle of men who put their bodies on the line for little more than pocket change, stomping around in a fantasy land. Most of the people who have paid are there in earnest, fans of the sport who look past the shoestring budget of tonight's program and simply wish to be entertained for an evening. The music blasts over the cheap, overwhelmed PA system. The lights begin to dim, and a pumped-up man's voice begins to announce tonight's card. It is five minutes to showtime.

Just behind the entrance curtain, Nick counts his wad of money, the incident with the child now far from his mind. Russell makes his way through the crowd of wrestlers milling about waiting for the show to start.

"You better hide that. Kurtis is looking for you. He wants to bust you and get us all kicked off the promotion." Russell casually tells Nick, who doesn't even look up from counting his money.

"Oh yeah, I know. I dosed him like an hour ago."

Russell takes a look around and spots Kurtis who is standing on his own about 20 feet from them. He is sweating profusely and staring at his hands that are held up in front of his face.

"WHAT THE FUCK ARE THEEEESE?!" Kurtis screams.

"He's gonna have a bad time," Nick says, smiling at Russell.

"You know, I've never actually tried acid before."

"Oh." Nick finally looks up at Russell while digging around in his pocket. "I have two left. Here you go."

Nick tosses a mostly empty ziplock bag to Russell.

"Are you sure?" Russell asks.

"Yeah. What will 16 hits do to me that 14 hits didn't?"

Russell holds it up and examines the two tabs of acid left in the bag. His eyes light up with familiarity.

"Oh, these things. I found some on the floor of the bathroom. That would explain all the . . . crazy things I've been seeing."

"You ate them . . . off of the floor?" A concerned Nick asks.

Russell brushes off the question; he is concerned about something in the crowd.

"Jesus, that guy looks fucking pisssssssed," Russell mutters under his breath.

A large, angry man with a VIP pass pushes his way through the crowd and towards Russell and Nick.

"Hey! Do you know which asshole showed my kid a picture of a fucking dead person?!" The man asks frantically.

Without hesitation, Nick points towards Kurtis, who is motionless and staring into space.

"That fucking pervert, right there!" Nick exclaims.

The large angry man smiles crazily and thanks Nick with a solid pat on the shoulder. With his fists already cocked and his eyes full of fire and rage, he stomps off in Kurtis' direction.

He passes Adam, who is now decked out in a feather boa, expensive-looking mirrored sunglasses, and white gloves. He dramatically stops in front of the men and strikes a contrapposto pose. The two men look on, in awe.

"Escalating pageantry," Russell says, finally understanding the concept.

"You got it," Adam replies, breaking the pose. The men all laugh as if this is the corny ending to a sitcom. The laughter peters out quickly, however.

"I'm too fucking high to wrestle," Adam declares confidently.

"Me too," Russell adds, nodding his head.

"I've been too high all day," Nick tells the guys.

Russell slips the last two hits of acid on his tongue. It's going to be an interesting night at the Samantha Martin Memorial curling rink.

From beyond the entrance curtain, the first match is announced. The crowd cheers, and the show begins.

OUR OLD BASS PLAYER WOKE UP FROM A COMA WITH PSYCHIC POWERS. YOU'RE OUT OF THE BAND

Listen, we all knew it was a matter of time. As you know, a few weeks ago Daryll woke up from his five-year coma. We were all positively STOKED for our bro. He has truly been to "the other side" of life (some say death) and it wasn't long before he began asking about getting into the jamspot and raging on some bangers again. It was a little hazy at first, but it is clear now that Daryll came back from the void with some strange gifts. Yes, he levitates now. Yes, if he grabs your hands, he can see the future. Yes, he woke up with the ability to flawlessly execute "Nobody Weird Like Me" by the Red Hot Chili Peppers. You should have seen his eyes, red with both tears and literal visions of an apocalyptic future, when we told him you had replaced him in the band. He was crushed, and I don't just mean his lower half from his garbage truck injury. When he and I were ready, he grabbed my hand tightly, went to "the other place," and saw visions of what the band would be if he rejoined. More about that later.

In the five years since you joined our musical journey, we in "The Pussy Men" have learned a lot from you, but I feel like we have also taught you. For instance, we've taught you how to play "Nobody Weird Like Me" by the Red Hot Chili Peppers like 600 times, but you still can't seem to grasp it. You laugh it off when you screw it up, and we laugh too, but that's just out of awkwardness and being too nice to say anything negative on our part. You have confidence issues and you should work that out before continuing on with your musical career. Yes, we've rocked bangers, destroyed the biggest talent shows, and packed every hotel bar in this backwater town, but it's time for us to separate so that "The Pussy Men" can actualize our true destiny. We're the big fish in the small pond. Maybe we should have spent the last five years touring or promoting or writing our own songs, but hindsight is 20/20. Daryll's future sight from his third eye is even better, though.

That night in the hospital, with his hand clamped around mine and eyes rolling back into his head, he told me the future of the band. It was an intense reading. He shook wildly. Objects moved on their own through the air. The door to the bathroom opened and slammed violently. We should have posted it to Instagram, but sadly my girlfriend Becky is on the rag and picked that moment to tell me I always boss her around. Classic Becky. Daryll spoke in a foreign, heavily articulated whisper. I wrote down what I could make out, and bro, things are really looking up for us. Well, not you, but you know what I mean. He spoke of a time of endless famine from a red hot sun where the blogs are diggin' us like CRAZY. In this world he speaks of, the rain is poison and the dead are disposed of in mass graves, but there is some label interest and it sounds like the industry is finally starting to notice us. Four-figure music videos, 90's-era Bon Jovi comparisons and eight days on/two days off from the vicious heat of the solar fields. It seems like it's all coming up Pussy Men, and sorry buddy, you just aren't going to be a part of it.

In his clearest, most powerful vision he did mention something interesting. He saw you. Your face perpetually dirt-stained from the years of sparring and losing in an apocalyptic battle with our climate. Your clothes are standard-issue water mining gear, not uncommon for a typical labourer. On your sleeve is a heavily worn black band signifying yet another death of your fellow crewmen. You don't even bother to take it off anymore, because in this future you are constantly in a state of mourning. Your head moves back and forth. Your body sways to the beat. On stage, "The Pussy Men" rip through a flawless cover of "Nobody Weird Like Me" by the Red Hot Chili Peppers. A smile crosses your face. For just a moment, everything is alright.

But for now, your shit is on the front porch. Come get it whenever.

A.I. OR A GAS LEAK? WHAT'S SUPER CHARGING MY PRODUCTIVITY?

Something amazing is happening.

It started, like so many things, innocently. It was day 15 of my uptick in productivity when a loud thud woke me up around noon. I was tightly grasping an armful of bathroom tiles. I didn't know where they came from, but I didn't feel concerned. I said out loud to myself, *trust the process*.

I had needed a change, that much was clear. I was sitting in a coffee shop with a friend who was telling me about the novel he had written with something called Artificial Intelligence.

"A sexual thriller made by this?" I said, motioning toward the grey box he called a computer. He turned it towards me, and I executed my first prompt: *How far apart are my eyes?* I watched the cursor blink a few times before responding back with Yes.

"Amazing," I said to myself. When I looked up to share my joy, I noticed he was gone. I was not in a coffee shop. There was a weird beeping alarm going off near the furnace. Oh well, no time for that. I had things to get done.

Is this machine learning from me, or am I learning from it? It's an amazing time to be alive when this technology is free and available from this grey box. The smell of rotten eggs emanating from the basement of my house was making me hungry. I realized I was sick of my diet.

The machine had the solutions. I've been eating peanut-butter-covered hunks of drywall, and the macros are simply insane. My creativity has seen a boost since it suggested I watch old TV shows and write an obituary for every dog I see. It advised that I use the word plutocrat, and ever since then, everything is a plutocrat.

Are there drawbacks? Of course. Every breakthrough has them. I am dizzy from excitement, I have headaches from solving so many problems, I am nauseous from setting and clearing goals, and I am also having difficulty breathing which I am struggling to connect to a positive outcome of my A.I. use.

By the third day, the shrill, beeping, alarmist-type sounds from various parts of my house had died down, and I could do some serious thinking. I was locked in. But nothing happens in a vacuum, and I found myself craving some social interaction. I asked the computer for some interesting news it had heard recently, and it mentioned that a group of Dutch scientists had stopped aging in mice.

“I'm like a mice!” I exclaimed, pumping my fist in the air. I was standing in front of my computer. I was naked. I was woohooing. I was apexing. I looked around my house and thought, It's time for an upgrade.

I know what you are thinking. How did you not know you had a gas leak? Well, honestly, I figured it out when I realized the computer hadn't been plugged in for days. But I liked it. The gas-leak/A.I. tandem was working in my favour. For once, I had the advantage. I was not going to let it go.

I had the devil in me, and the devil was an unwieldy combination of noxious gas and machine learning. But it made me fly too close to the sun.

The thud that woke me up that morning—the one where I was clutching the bathroom tiles was the beginning of the end. I cracked open the door to investigate the sound and found my tonnage of soybeans, which I had ordered, being delivered. The A.I. instructed me to invest, and the gas leak demanded I diversify.

Due to a confused flour beetle infestation, soybean values had plummeted. I just needed a place to store my soybeans until the market bounced back and I could trade them for the fine, fine silver the gas leak had demanded. I instructed the men to load the beans onto the lawn, but as they drove away, I felt the drops of the worst-case scenario start to pitter-patter on my head. The rain was coming.

Earlier in the day, I had asked the computer/the gas leak what the weather was going to be, but it only repeated the word Spaghetti over and over again. I had nodded my head in agreement, which only now seems foolish. I opened the door and ran to salvage my investment. I started to fill my pockets with beans, shoved them in my mouth, created a basket with my T-shirt, and filled it. I did this a few times until I had a sudden, inexplicable moment of clarity.

My dizziness subsided. My head stopped hurting. My nausea finally passed, and I was able to take a deep breath. I looked down at the rocks and dirt falling through my fingers. There were no beans. There never were.

I was naked. I was not woohooing. I was certainly not apexing.

The door had been open long enough that by the time the fire department arrived, they were able to fix the leak fairly quickly. No one would make eye contact with me as they left my "Productivity Centre." The drywall had been ripped off the walls and eaten, the sandwich meat I had been sleeping on had gone bad, and my crème brûlées had all split in the oven.

The computer I had been using all this time had been a dissatisfied-looking turtle. She was angry. I was angry. Truthfully, the world of the gas was just easier. It was easier to exist in the arms of its frantic ups than in the reality of constant downs.

I walked downstairs past my half-finished projects: the alcohol still I had created out of my toilet, the toilet I had created out of the alcohol still, past my copy of *Atlas Shrugged* and my copy of *Atlas Shrugged* that I had been using as a toilet. I made my way further into the madness until I found the pilot light.

I took a deep breath in, the last unproductive breath I would ever take again, and blew out the flame.

Hello, apex.

NEW PAINT COLOURS FOR OUR FAILING REPUBLIC

OMG, fall is here and with it the complete and utter collapse of our democracy! Your face might be a touch drab and colourless, as if the only light that has touched your skin is the blue one from your phone screen as you doomscroll and softly whisper *what the fuck over* and over, but that doesn't mean your walls couldn't use a splash of colour! Let's put to rest our existential dread and put to use those rock-hard brushes and drop sheets that are sitting in that dusty basement, because that is where you will have to build a hidden wall to hide your children when they come.

Up first is Sherwin-Williams with a new theme called *The Changes You Will Experience in the Coming Months*. I love it! These colours are fantastic tension builders. *Ponder* is up first. It's a flexible grey that will really make you think *How did we get here?* And *are you fucking kidding me?* It works well on its own or as an accent to a bolder choice such as *Complicit Grey*, a colour that helps you reconcile the thoughts that you figured someone was going to do something about all this, but it wasn't going to be you. Why accent a grey with a grey? Because, frankly, it's the end of the world, money is fake, and nothing matters anymore. Put these in a bedroom and you can stare at the walls for hours while chewing your nails until your stomach hurts.

Marooned is another highlight; it has a real "arrested but charged with no crime" vibe. *Increasingly Empty Store Shelves* and *Fighting Over Baby Formula* might be a few derivatives of similar darker shades, but the collection is saved by *Distant News*, an impressive deep red that will cover up any questions you might have about why you don't see a single dissenting opinion against the state in our once-fertile journalistic landscape. The possibilities for your colour journey!

But hold up — the old guard at the Behr paint company isn't just following orders with their latest swatch. Having trouble fitting the uber-sophisticated surveillance tool that you call a smart TV into your living room aesthetic? The ravishing, succulent tones found in *Observer* will offset that clunky hunk of plastic that monitors and catalogues every protesting word you say by incorporating it into part of the room's motif. *Unread Terms and Conditions* is a charming exterior off-white that pairs well with the Ring camera that will see your neighbour's entire family arrested for reasons you shouldn't concern yourself with. *Police or At Least I Think They Were the Police Because They Had Guns* is a new spin on the old dusty pink that harkens back to simple times when Nazis wore garish uniforms and not the camouflage of a helpful politician! Reflect on the way the sun kisses the flecks of silver in the paint as the men in masks with no visible identifiers demand you erase the footage of your neighbour's arrest. Sounds like spooky season is here to stay!

Cloverdale Paint might be the new kid on the block, but their colour lineup might be the only piece of information you'll see today that isn't disinformation. *The Rumbling of Tanks in Our Suburban Neighbourhood* says "Yes!" to a boot stamping on a human face forever, while *My Pharmacy Is on Fire and My Medication Will Only Last So Long* makes you feel something, and at this point you will take it. With only a few delicate strokes on the wall, *I Thought I'd Be Watching from the Sidelines* really captures the fear inherent in running toward a closed border while holding your screaming child with one hand and a few meagre possessions in the other, and let me tell you I'm absolutely gagging over it.

Which paint company? Which tones? Which shades? These are, frankly, gigantic questions to ask yourself in the modern décor battlefield. But what else are you going to do with your time? Endlessly Google which engine block will protect you from gunfire the best, or the shelf life of commonly found processed foods? Sounds grim! Throw some colour on your walls and express yourself in these last days of our once envied Republic. And if I may so, the colour of your clenched white knuckles would look good on the kitchen cabinets. If it were a colour, I think I'd call it *Inevitable*.

TOMORROW AND BACK AGAIN

It's the middle of the night, and the bus station is mostly empty. A lone figure with a wiry fro and a red duffel bag walks with purpose through the departures area and towards the toonie lockers. The figure opens one of the lockers and stuffs the duffel bag inside. He slams the locker door shut.

THE PRESENT

Steve sits at a table in a large warehouse. His wiry fro drips with sweat under the intense lights. In his mid-30s, he is a younger man than you'd think an inventor to be. His bulldog frame looks nice under the white lab coat he found at the thrift store, and his black, horn-rimmed glasses give him an intelligent look. He may not have gone to school like the other inventors of his time, but Steve possesses the same street smarts that Tesla, Edison and Marconi all had. Formal education took a backseat in Steve's life to his main passion: the drums. Throughout his teen years and early 20s, Steve spent his time devoted to the beat, playing in bands all across this great country. These aren't bar bands, mind you, thoughtlessly playing covers of other people's hit songs. Steve and his various musical companions were conceiving math rock gems, alt-rock adventures and alternative takedowns of the pop structure. Alas, as he grew older, he had to find a more stable career, and his true calling became clear: inventor.

Whatever Steve is putting together at this moment requires every ounce of his concentration. He twists wires, he solders, he drills, and he welds. He is doing complicated, delicate work. The wisp of colophony fume disappears into the air as he makes one last solder connection. He stops, puts down his tool and takes a moment to wipe the sweat from his brow with an old, dirty sock. The work is complete. Steve stares down at a red switch he has just finished wiring; this is the moment of truth. He licks his lips with anticipation as his finger moves slowly toward the switch. The tension in the room is on par with an executive decision to launch the missiles that will end all of humanity as we know it. He flicks the switch into the on position, and the room fills with the sound of an awful, giant, bombastic machine. Steve's latest invention is alive.

The machine he was working on is merely a mannequin hand that has been hollowed out and attached to an electric turkey cutter. It pumps up and down, simulating furious masturbation. Steve stands over the table, his palms flat on the surface, examining the machine from all angles, no matter how absurd that might be. He pulls a small notepad out of his breast pocket and quickly scratches down a few rough notes. “Nail polish?” he writes, adding several dots beside it for emphasis.

Satisfied, Steve places the invention on a shelf marked *“Masturbatory Aids: Second Drafts”* next to a Ziplock bag of pumpkin filling and the ill-fated *“garden shear/penis pump hybrid,”* which Steve has a good feeling about. Although it seems hopeless in the present, he has plans to revisit it in the future.

Across from the wall of shelves is a giant calendar mounted to the wall. It is at least seven feet tall. All the days have activities marked on them, and the days that have passed have X's through them. Today, February 5th, 2015, "crude sex toy" is written in the AM portion of the calendar. Steve carefully crosses it out and takes a step back to look at the calendar as a whole. The days, the activities, the future, and the past. Under the recently crossed-out activity on today's date, the words "TRAVEL THROUGH TIME" are written in bold letters in the PM section. Steve nods his head.

Pulling off a large tarp, Steve unveils his interdimensional chariot. It is a pedal-powered device that, to the layman, would appear to be nothing more than a stationary bike covered with Christmas lights and cheap handmade wings mounted onto either side. The control panel appears to consist of several reappropriated calculators and digital timekeepers, incorporated as devices to set a date to travel to, as well as latitude and longitude to pinpoint your location upon arrival in the past or future. It was crude and rudimentary but had taken almost two full Sundays to hone and build. Steve ran his hands along the frame, imagining the adventures he was about to embark on. Perhaps he would see the birth of Christ or the death of the universe, but today's plans were more humble: An afternoon, just a bit in the future.

Steve sets the location parameters and types in the date 02 05 2016, one year from today. He straps on a leather helmet and a pair of vintage aviator glasses. He hops on the bike and begins to pedal, slowly at first, but he soon picks up speed as the wings begin to flap. Hitting his stride, Steve honks a horn that's connected to the bike. *"AOOOGAH!!!"* The horn shouts. Pedalling like a man possessed, Steve begins breathing hard. He grinds his teeth as sparks begin jumping from the instrument panel. Something is happening; it's possible the bike might explode as the frame shakes and the belt on the tire groans with effort. A flash illuminates from the bike, lighting up the entire warehouse. Outside, two homeless gentlemen congregating in front of an oil drum fire see the immense flash of light emanating from the windows of the warehouse.

"Looks like ol' Mr. McNeil be up to sumthin, and I don't think it's a pocket pussy," Maurice, one of the hobos, remarks.

"Mmmhmm," answers Charles, the other hobo. "I believe he is dabblin' in something he doesn't quite understand..."

The two men stare at each other for a moment before launching into a pitch-perfect acapella version of *"It's My Life"* by Bon Jovi.

THE FUTURE

"Wake up, you dirty motherfucker! I ain't telling you again!"

The words are like a cold bucket of water on Steve's head. He jolts up from his unconscious state. The voice belongs to a man in a janitor's outfit. It seems that the custodian has been nice enough to clean around Steve's sleeping body, but the time has come to clean around the toilet in the public bathroom, and that's exactly where Steve's head was, passed out face down and drooling on the floor. Steve, still out of it, is confused at first. He hasn't woken up in a bathroom stall in a few years, and he doesn't feel like he has taken magic mushrooms, yet there is a large wet piss stain on the crotch of his pants, so he couldn't rule out a psilocybin adventure entirely.

"The time machine!" Steve blurts out, it all coming back to him in an instant.

"Time what?" The janitor asks. Steve lunges out and grabs the janitor by the collar of his overalls like a drowning man grasping for a line to pull him in.

"What day is it? The date?!" Steve frantically asks the man.

The janitor easily pushes Steve's hands off of him.

"5th . . . February . . . Friday," The janitor answers.

"THE YEAR!?" Steve demands.

The janitor drops his broom, his hands go up in a defensive position and he begins to back away from Steve.

"I don't know what freaky shit you got up to, mister, but you got piss all over you, and I think you shit your pants. I don't want any part of it."

The janitor backs himself out of the door. Steve looks down at his soiled pants and sighs. Has he traveled through time? Or was this merely another blackout? The type that has become so common since he started his radiation tests.

"But these are the exact coordinates.." Steve mutters to himself.

He knows there is something special about this room. In his previous tests, he'd only time-travelled a few minutes into the future and felt fine, but a whole year has left him disoriented and foggy. His head feels like it is spinning. He lays back down on the floor.

"Something about this room..." He says to himself.

Absentmindedly turning his head, he sees something unusual underneath the sink.

"That's it!" Steve exclaims.

In a second, he is up and making his way to the sink. He reaches underneath and grabs the object that jump-started his memory: a locker key labelled C14.

Steve makes his way out of the bathroom and into the busy main area of the bus terminal. The hustle and bustle of the afternoon crowd seems ordinary to him. Feeling weak, he stops by a trash can to get his bearings. Taking a few breaths he notices a freshly-discarded half eaten ice cream cone just under the rim of the can.

"Wherever I am, people are still wasteful," He says to himself, shaking his head. He picks the ice cream cone out of the garbage and begins to eat it.

Feeling recharged from the sugar, Steve cuts through the crowd and toward the lockers by the departure gate. He slips the key into locker C14 and opens it, finding a red duffel bag. He pulls it out and shuts the locker.

Having found a dark corner of the underground parkade of the bus station, Steve begins to go through the contents of the bag. He first grabs an envelope that has "READ FIRST" written in large, bold letters. He tears it open to find a letter from himself.

Dear future Steve,

If you're reading this, that means our experiment was a success. I've packed in this duffel bag enough supplies for your journey. I hope the clothes I've picked out are still as fashionable in your time as they are in mine.

Steve pulls out a pair of khaki pants, a plaid button-up shirt and a logoless black zip-up hoodie. They are the exact clothes that he is wearing already, minus the large, now slightly dried piss stain. He changes into the new duds and continues reading the letter.

I've also supplied you with 5 grams of marijuana to calm your nerves.

Reaching into the bag, Steve produces a film roll with the familiar insignia of a crudely drawn pot leaf on the top.

"Sweet," Steve says to himself.

He opens the container and dumps it into his hand, but instead of feeling the expected weight of a few hearty nugs, only a few scraps of paper fall out and into his hand. All of the pieces of paper have *"IOU some weed"* written on them. Steve is disappointed but shrugs, knowing he'd do the same thing.

I'm not sure about the political climate of your time, so I've packed you some gold kuager...kruger - ants? Kruger Some gold coins.

Steve unzips a blue banker's bag. Once again, it is full of pieces of paper with *"IOU some gold coins."* At the bottom of the banker's bag is eight dollars in toonies.

"Eight bucks?" Steve says, confused. He begins double-checking the banker's bag again. "That's killer!" He puts the toonies in his pocket.

He continues digging through the bag, and this time, he pulls out a handgun. He handles it with surprising expertise, ejecting and inserting the magazine from the Glock to check if it is loaded. He slips the handgun into the back of his pants and continues reading the letter.

The future can be a dangerous place, so I've provided you with some protection.

I can't guarantee that I've sent you to the right place or the right time. But you must get back to the time machine by 8pm tonight. Be careful of what you do. If you change the future too much, time will snap back like a rubber band. Don't do anything drastic unless you have to. If something isn't right, don't worry, in the end, it will all make sense.

Love,

Future Steve.

After packing the various items back into the duffel bag, Steve sets the alarm on his trusty digital watch for 7:59 pm.

Walking out of the bus station parkade, Steve finds himself in the world of the future. Technically. A year isn't really a mind-blowing amount of time to travel to, to be honest. He went to his favourite restaurant, and all the regular employees and customers were still there. His favourite meal is still on the menu and still tastes the same. That carpet store that was having a going-out-of-business sale went out of business and has been replaced by another carpet store that's having a going-out-of-business sale. He surveys the new technology at the local electronic store, but everything is basically the same. He encounters one odd thing. Going by his warehouse space, his key no longer fits into the lock. *"In the end, it will all make sense,"* the letter had said.

"It's best not to worry too much about it until I come back tonight," he says to himself, trying to shrug off his worrisome feelings.

"Is that you? Steven McNeil?" a raspy voice calls out to Steve as he inspects the lock on the warehouse. He turns to see Maurice and Charles, the two homeless gentlemen that usually hung around the warehouse singing by an oil drum. They are stunned to see Steve. It was Maurice that called out, but Steve knew that smooth baritone anywhere.

"Maurice! How are you?" Steve calls back at them; the two men are about 20 feet away and seem to be keeping their distance.

"We be sorry, sir, we won't be trespassin' again, sir!" Charles calls out while grabbing Maurice's arm, trying to pull him by the coat away from Steve.

"Trespassing? That's strange," Steve thinks to himself. He has never given either of the men any guff for trespassing on the grounds of the warehouse. In fact, he quite enjoys their company. Being an inventor can be a lonely life, and Maurice and Charles are always up for a late-night jam or to try out Steve's latest masturbatory aids. No one dared to fuck a Ziplock bag full of pumpkin filling until Maurice showed up that rainy night, and his contributions to the project have been vital.

"You lookin' well, sir, back to normal even!" Maurice calls out to him while being pulled by Charles.

"Back to normal?" Steve asks himself. What does that mean? Looking at his watch, he only has a few hours to kill before going back in time, but with the cold of the night creeping up on him and no way into the warehouse as of yet, he decides to make his way back into the city and see if he can figure out what these hobos are talking about.

The walk back to the city's metropolitan area had given him a few moments to think about himself and this travelling through time business. Steve knows he has a passion for inventing, and yes, maybe his engineering skills aren't up to par, but raw skill and imagination are a good bedrock for an inventor's career. He's sure the showmanship and polish will come with time, but he must say, he's thoroughly impressed with his ability to build a device that can travel through time. He had only been at the inventing gig for about nine months, and aside from his boorish masturbatory aids, which, in the inventing field, is akin to the phrase *"any idiot can melt cheese",* that is to say, it is an easy field to excel at, he has created the ability to travel to and manipulate time as he sees fit.

That's where the self-congratulation for the project ended, and the fear began. If he can honestly stumble onto time travel while fixing a stationary bike, what is stopping anyone else? What if their intentions aren't as pure as his?

Why are Maurice and Charles so hesitant to speak to him? Even trying to get away from him? Upon his return to the present, the time machine must be destroyed.

Walking down the street, lost in thought, a gentle, familiar melody drifts into Steve's ear. He can't put his finger on where he knows it from. The notes of the saxophone are partially lost in the cool wind, but Steve begins filling in the gaps with a gentle hum. As he approaches the source of the sound, either a busker or some other kind of street performer, he realizes where he recognizes the song from: It's one he had written.

Several years ago, he had played drums in a four- or five-piece (depending on the day and who was available in the decidedly unorganized and unreliable group) garage rock band called "The Pink Coats." The only song worth a damn was one that Steve had written called *"Translucent Days."* The main part of the song was a simple 5-note melody in a minor key, and that's what he is hearing right now. Normally, Steve would be flattered at such a homage, but *"Translucent Days"* had never been recorded, and The Pink Coats had never played a gig before breaking up. How does this person know Steve's obscure song?

It's mid-afternoon, and the pedestrian-only street bustles with foot traffic: shoppers lugging around oversized bags of merchandise, business people going from meeting to meeting, and street entertainers hustling to make a buck. Steve focuses on following the melancholy sound of the saxophone back to its origins. As he crosses the busy street, he finally lays his eyes on his target. The man has his back to Steve but is dressed in what looks to be the tightest, most uncomfortable pair of leather pants he has ever seen. He also sports a black mesh crop top shirt. The man's wiry fro is partially stuffed under a top hat.

"This doesn't look like anyone who would know a Pink Coats tune, that's for sure," Steve mumbles to himself.

Stays at the perimeter and out of sight of the saxophonist, Steve gets the feeling that something isn't right about all this. The constant stream of people makes it difficult to see the man's face, and before Steve knows it, the man has stopped playing and is putting his instrument away into a snug-fitting case. Steve blends in with the throng of people and manages to position himself to see the man's face once and for all. The man is still kneeling, but having put away the saxophone, he is now collecting the change that strangers toss him.

"Just one look. Who is this thief?" Steve says to himself.

Finally, the man stands up. A pause in the foot traffic leaves Steve and the saxophonist just ten feet apart and in full view of each other. The two men lock eyes for a moment. Steve's mouth hangs open in amazement, unable to speak. The saxophonist turns on his heels and runs into the crowd of people.

It couldn't be. But it's possible. But it couldn't be.

Working his way through the crowd, Steve stays hot on the trail of the mysterious man who is now bringing to light all the fears Steve had been thinking about just moments ago.

"Hey, hold up a second!" Steve yells to him.

The man doesn't let up. He darts in and out of people's way, walking against the flow of foot traffic, trying to put as much distance between the two men as possible. Steve, meanwhile, is forced to be less than polite while trying to keep up with him, leaving a trail of sorries and gosh-I-apologize in his wake.

The mysterious man ducks into an alleyway off of the pedestrian-only street. Steve follows, but the man seems to have vanished. He cautiously makes his way into the alley, his hand inside his hoodie and on the handle of his gun. If this is what Steve thinks it is, it could get ugly. A piece of paper catches Steve's eye as it floats by and drifts down towards his feet. It is a flyer for a local rock concert. Steve leans down and picks it up.

"What . . . the . . . fuck?" Steve says.

Without warning, Steve is struck from behind with something heavy. He falls to the ground, unconscious. Standing over him, the mysterious man picks up the ratty piece of paper Steve had been looking at. The flyer is for a club performance by *"The World's Premiere Goth Saxophonist, Steve McNeil."* The picture of Steve on the flyer shows him to be tricked out in heavy goth wear; he has a pencil goatee, guyliner, and a lot of foundation. His fro is tied in a topknot, and he wears a mesh shirt. He blows into a saxophone and looks really "cool."

"You're right on time, my friend," future Steve whispers into Steve's unconscious ear.

His psychotic laugh echoes through the empty alleyway as the sun sets and the cold begins to set in. However, it peters out quickly, and he begins to rummage through Steve's pockets.

"I wonder if he has any weed."

Steve wakes up in an industrial garbage bin. His head aches from the blow he sustained, and there is a small amount of blood mashed into his fro. He pulls himself out of the garbage can and dusts himself off, he sighs, noticing he has once again pissed his pants.

"No time travel to blame for that one . . ." he says to himself, embarrassed.

Just then Steve notices the alley that he finds himself in is bathed in darkness.

"The time!' he frantically looks at his watch to find it is already 7:32 pm.

"I gotta get back to the warehouse! Back to my own time!"

Finding the warehouse door unlocked, Steve pulls open the large metal doors. He has made it back with little time to spare. Who knows what would happen if he got stuck here, stuck with this mysterious goth version of himself? Steve draws his handgun. The future can be a dangerous place, after all.

Slowly making his way into the main workroom, Steve's heart sinks. The time machine lies in pieces on the floor—belts cut, lights broken, wings torn off and even the frame is deconstructed. Someone knows what they're doing to make sure that Steve doesn't get back, and the list of suspects is only one name long.

"Why'd you do this to me?" Steve asks the darkened corners of the warehouse.

"So we can take over the world," a voice answers back.

Stepping out of the shadows rather loudly due to the number of jingling accessories and leather he is wearing, Future Steve appears. Steve lets the gun drop to his side.

There is no reason to kill him; revenge would be a pointless exercise.

"What do you mean *take over the world*? You destroyed the time machine," Steve asks meekly.

"We're not gonna use time, baby," Future Steve raises his driving-glove-clad hand and snaps his fingers three times. "We're gonna use music. You and I are gonna create the world's greatest band. I'll front it, and you'll play the drums."

Steve is confused.

"You created a time paradox so we could make a band together?" Steve asks.

"Baby, it's like what you always said, *'If there was just another me in this band . . .'* Well, now there is." Future Steve gestures to himself in all his gothed-out glory. He continues, "No more flakes not showing up to practice interrupting with their stupid ideas and their stupid thoughts. No more arguments over band names or pay. I've spent the last year planning it all out. Singing lessons, saxophone lessons. I took a sophisticated Stage Presence course from Berkley. I travelled the globe finding the latest killer fashions, as you can see." Steve points to his long black leather coat and platform boots."

"Uhhh, okay," Steve says, seemingly warming up to the idea. "Do you have some songs, or—"

"That's the beautiful part, baby," Future Steve interrupts. "That's the whole plan. I used the time machine to go forward in time, and I figured out what the most popular cover songs are going to be for the next ten years."

Future Steve unveils a whiteboard with ten of the world's most popular cover songs written on it.

"Covers! We're gonna play covers?!" Steve yells. He raises the gun up to Future Steve once again. Maybe this suggestion is actually worth killing him for?

"Oh please, Mr. Morals. Mr. Integrity. What do you have against covers?" Future Steve asks snidely.

"It's lazy and stupid!" Steve replies. "Anyone can play covers! You gotta write the song, man. It's gotta come from inside." Steve uses the gun to gesture to his heart.

"Oh please," Future Steve huffs. "What have you ever gotten from writing songs? Money? A career? No, you got bills. Bills from the jam space owner, bills from the guy who records your song, bills from the guy who mixes the song, bills from the artsy twat you hire to make a music video that you don't even like. Everyone gets rich off musicians except musicians!"

Steve lowers the gun again. Future Steve is making a pretty good case.

"You really think we can make some money doing this?" Steve asks.

"It'll be like money you've never seen before, my sweet Steven. And that's just the start. The pussy, Steve. Pussy so hot your momma will have to put it on the window sill to cool it off before you eat it."

"Jesus," Steve says, shocked at how vulgar he has become in the past year.

"That was a bit fucked up, I'll admit it. But nonetheless. It's what you've always wanted."

Steve begins to nod his head. Is it time to go to the dark side? To form the cover band? Steve looks at the whiteboard again. Something is off.

"Wait . . ."

"It's a brilliant list, isn't it?" Future Steve asks.

"I know all these songs."

"Yeah, hence their universal appeal." Future Steve smugly admires the whiteboard.

"You went ten years into the future to figure out the best cover songs?" Steve points to a few songs on the list. "The Chicken Dance? Sweet Caroline? Why didn't you just steal hit songs from the future and record them first?"

Future Steve ponders this for a second.

"Hmmm . . . that is . . . a better . . . idea. Well, we can just use the time machine—" Future Steve gestures towards the smashed time machine on the ground. "Oh fuck. Yeah. Fuck." Future Steve looks around for a second, trying to improvise an idea. He quickly gives up. "I have to stop smoking so much fuckin' weed, man."

Steve lets out a deep sigh as his mind begins to race. There's not a chance that he will be trapped in the future with this gothic imbecile to play in a low-rent cover band. He thought back to the letter he had written himself.

"Don't do anything drastic unless you have to."

"I gotta chill for a while, man. You got any weed left?" Future Steve asks, a hint of desperation in his voice.

Steve knows what he has to do. He raises his gun to Future Steve's chest.

"What are you doing, man?" Future Steve asks, scared, raising his hands.

"I have to do something drastic."

"Come on, man, I just got this jacket off of layaway," Future Steve pleads.

"I'm sorry," Steve whispers. He closes his eyes, the pistol shaking in his hands.

"I don't want to kill you aga—"

Future Steve calls out as Steve squeezes the trigger.

As the bullet passes through Future Steve's heart, a bright light emanates through the hole in his chest. Steve drops the gun, but it doesn't fall. The gun has now been absorbed by the light, as has Steve. The light begins to pour out of his eyes and mouth. He tries to scream, but there is no use. Soon the men, the warehouse and the inventions are all absorbed into the brilliant light. There is no future, no past and no present here. Time has died.

THE ?

Standing back in his warehouse, Steve's eyes adjust slowly back to the dim afternoon warehouse light. He quickly checks the crotch of his pants to find they are still dry. Odd.

Across the room, his past self pedals furiously on the stationary bike, breathless, momentum still driving his legs. He blinks at the fading white flash and at the sudden appearance of himself from the future. Steve locks eyes with Past Steve, who looks at the stool beside him where a revolver sits. Steve sees the gun as well, and he begins to make his way toward Past Steve, no words are able to leave his mouth before Past Steve, still on the bike, picks up the gun and shoots him dead.

Looking at the corpse of himself, Past Steve feels a strange detachment. This is not a person, just another failed, broken experiment laying on his warehouse floor.

The smell of cordite still burning in his nose, Past Steve walks into the dank, filthy warehouse bathroom. He puts the gun down on the sink and opens the mirrored medicine cabinet. There, sitting on one of the long-neglected shelves, is some black eyeliner. Steve grabs it and closes the mirror cabinet. He takes a long look at himself in the mirror. Maybe it's time for a change. He screws the top off of the eyeliner container and begins to apply it judiciously.

It's the middle of the night, and the bus station is mostly empty. A lone figure with a wiry fro and a red duffel bag walks with purpose through the departures area and towards the toonie lockers. The figure opens one of the lockers and stuffs the duffel bag in it. He slams the locker door shut. Past Steve walks out of the bus station. The cold air blows through his long leather jacket, through the mesh shirt and through the various beads twisted into his goatee. He slips on his black sunglasses.

"The future is here, at last," he says to himself.

ABOUT THE AUTHOR

Rob White is a writer based in Regina whose work blends humour, melancholy, and the surreal. He has written essays and short comedic pieces for outlets such as *Points in Case, Slackjaw, The Bear Creek Gazette* and *Little Old Lady Comedy*. In 2025, Rob had the unlikely pleasure of opening for David Sedaris on his Canadian tour.

Rob is also a filmmaker who's award winning films have been screened internationally and his work has been featured on *Vice, Noisey, Business Insider,* and *The Hard Times*.

Manufactured by Amazon.ca
Bolton, ON

55963922R00133